STAR-CROSSED

candy apple books...
just for you.
sweet. fresh. fun.
take a bite!

The Accidental Cheerleader by Mimi McCoy

The Boy Next Door by Laura Dower

Miss Popularity by Francesco Sedita

How to Be a Girly Girl in Just Ten Days
by Lisa Papademetriou

Drama Queen by Lara Bergen

The Babysitting Wars by Mimi McCoy

Totally Crushed by Eliza Willard

I've Got a Secret by Lara Bergen

Callie for President by Robin Wasserman

Making Waves by Randi Reisfeld and H. B. Gilmour

The Sister Switch
by Jane B. Mason and Sarah Hines Stephens

Accidentally Fabulous by Lisa Papademetriou

Confessions of a Bitter Secret Santa by Lara Bergen

Accidentally Famous by Lisa Papademetriou

STAR-CROSSED

by MIMI McCOY

candy
apple

SCHOLASTIC INC.

New York   Toronto   London   Auckland   Sydney
Mexico City   New Delhi   Hong Kong   Buenos Aires

No part of this publication may be
reproduced, stored in a retrieval system,
or transmitted in any form or by any means,
electronic, mechanical, photocopying, recording,
or otherwise, without written permission of the publisher.
For information regarding permission, write to Scholastic Inc.,
557 Broadway, New York, NY 10012.

ISBN-13: 978-0-545-04666-4
ISBN-10: 0-545-04666-1

12 11 10 9 8 7 6 5 4 3 2 1   9 10 11 12 13 14/0
Printed in the U.S.A.   40

First printing, February 2009

Thanks to my sister, Elyse, for
her middle-school insights;
to Catherine and Greg
for their helpful suggestions;
and to James Presnell
for his track advice.

⋆ *Chapter One* ⋆

The last-period bell jangled through the halls of McKinley Middle School, signaling the end of the school day. A second later, the doors of the classrooms burst open, and kids flooded the halls, talking and laughing.

Abby Waterman was spinning the combination on her locker when her best friend, Chelsea Rinaldi, came hurrying up to her, her lips pursed in a secretive smile.

"I know that look," Abby said, her long blond hair swinging over one shoulder as she turned to study her friend. "You just saw Nathan again."

Chelsea's lips stretched into a full grin that showed her deep dimples. "He looked at me for, like, three full seconds," she told Abby. "That's the third time today!"

"It must be true love," Abby teased. Nathan Butcher was a seventh grader, and Chelsea had been crushing on him for almost the whole school year.

"Hey, can you come with me for a minute?" Chelsea asked Abby. "I have something I need to check."

"Now?" said Abby, putting her books into her locker. "But I have to get to track practice."

"It'll only take a second," Chelsea told her. "You're my best friend. I need moral support."

"Okay, I guess I have a little time," Abby said with a smile. Sometimes she still couldn't believe how lucky she was to have a best friend like Chelsea. When Abby had started sixth grade back in September, she hadn't known a soul. She and her parents had just moved to town, and though Abby was usually up for new things, the first day of school had been terrifying. McKinley was much, *much* bigger than her old school, and most of the kids seemed to already know each other. She'd been afraid she wouldn't have *any* friends — much less one as pretty and popular as Chelsea.

But her locker was right next to Chelsea's, and right away Chelsea had taken Abby under her wing. Chelsea had an instinct for how things worked in middle school, maybe because she had an older sister who'd already been through McKinley. From the beginning, Chelsea had known which tables to sit at in the cafeteria, which teachers would believe you if you said your computer ate your homework, and how to dress so you looked cool without seeming like you were trying. Abby could still remember Chelsea's first-day outfit: black Capri pants, a sleeveless striped shirt, and a cute red headband in her dark curly hair. It had looked fresh and casual, without seeming too trendy. Abby had shown up in baggy jeans, a T-shirt, and her favorite beat-up Converse low-tops. But with Chelsea's help, she'd updated her wardrobe — she still wore the sneakers, but now she paired them with stylish jeans and cute tops.

"So where are we going?" Abby asked as they walked down the hall together.

"The library," Chelsea told her.

"The library? No wonder you wanted moral support," Abby joked. Studying wasn't exactly Chelsea's thing. She was more into the three G's — Gossip, Guys, and lip Gloss — than the three R's.

The library was quiet and empty. The librarian, sorting books behind her desk, was the only person in sight. Chelsea walked right past her, making a beeline for the computers in the back of the room.

"What are you looking up?" Abby asked as they sat down in front of one of the monitors.

"My horoscope," Chelsea told her. "I didn't get a chance to check it this morning. We were late leaving for school, and Mom was on my case."

"Your horoscope?" Abby looked at her in surprise. "You really believe in that stuff?"

"Totally." Chelsea was busy typing in a Web address. A moment later, a Web site came up. Little gold moons and stars floated across a deep-blue background. Across the top in scrolling gold letters it read: MIZ ASTRID BRINGS THE STARS DIRECT 2 U!

Chelsea clicked on an icon of a little ram's head. "I can't look," she said, covering her eyes. "You read it to me."

Abby didn't get what all the drama was about, but she leaned over and read, "'Aries (March 21–April 20). You should have lots of mental focus today. If you're falling behind in something, now's the time to buckle down and get to work.'"

"That's it?" Chelsea uncovered her eyes and read the page herself. "What a lame horoscope," she said with a sigh.

"What did you think it was going to say?" Abby asked.

"I was *hoping* it would say something about Nathan. After we connected in the hall today, I thought maybe today's the day! But all this is telling me is that I'd better do my math homework tonight."

"How do you get that?" Abby asked, scanning the horoscope once more.

"I'm falling behind in math," Chelsea explained. "I've already missed three homework assignments."

"Oops," Abby said. That was one big difference between her and Chelsea — Abby always did her homework. "Well, you probably *should* get caught up," she told her friend. "But I wouldn't worry about your horoscope. I've heard this stuff is all just a bunch of baloney."

"It is not!" Chelsea gasped, her brown eyes widening. "I swear my horoscope comes true almost every day. Like yesterday, it said, 'You may have trouble with an authority figure.' And then last night my mom totally got on my case about cleaning up my room!"

"Hmm." Abby wasn't the kind of girl to burst her best friend's bubble, but it wasn't the most convincing argument. Chelsea's room was always messy, and Mrs. Rinaldi was always telling her to clean it up. "Well, what does *my* horoscope say?" she asked.

"Your birthday is October fifteenth, so . . . let's see. That makes you a Libra." Chelsea moused over the page until she came to an icon of a set of old-fashioned scales. She clicked on it, and Abby's horoscope popped up.

LIBRA (SEPTEMBER 23–OCTOBER 22)
UNEXPECTED RICHES MAY COME YOUR WAY TODAY. BUT YOU'D BE WISE TO AVOID THE OLD ADAGE "EASY COME, EASY GO." HANG ON TO YOUR NEWFOUND WEALTH FOR WHEN YOU REALLY NEED IT.

Abby laughed. "Unexpected riches, huh? Well, that just goes to show you it's not all true. I think I have about one dollar in my wallet."

"The day's not over yet." Chelsea wiggled her eyebrows mysteriously.

"R-i-i-ight." Abby rolled her eyes. "So, anyway, what did you mean when you said you wanted to know if today's the day? The day for what?"

"Well, you know the Spring Dance is next Friday, right?" Chelsea said.

Abby nodded. McKinley only had two dances a year — Fall and Spring — so they were kind of a big deal. Abby had already heard girls talking about what they were going to wear.

"I decided I'm going to ask Nathan," Chelsea told her. "But I want to do it on the right day, so he'll say yes."

"Wait a second. You're asking Nathan to the *dance*?" Abby was stunned. Usually Chelsea just talked *about* her crushes. She didn't talk *to* them — much less ask them out!

"Didn't you hear?" Chelsea said. "This year it's girl-ask-boy."

"Yeah, but . . ." Abby had heard that the dance was girl-ask-boy, but until now it hadn't occurred to her that *she* might have to ask someone. "I thought we would all just go in a big group, like we did in the fall," she said.

In October, Abby, Chelsea, and a bunch of other sixth grade girls had all gotten ready for the Fall Dance together, then they'd had a slumber party afterward. It had been a blast. Abby had been looking forward to doing it again for the Spring Dance.

But Chelsea shook her head. "The Fall Dance is just casual. But the Spring Dance is dress-up. You have to have a date for a dress-up dance. Everyone knows that."

"Oh." Abby hadn't known that. She'd come from a small, private school for grades one through eight, and they hadn't had any dances there. Even though she'd been at McKinley for as long as Chelsea had, Abby still sometimes felt like the new girl.

"So you haven't thought about who you're going to ask?" Chelsea said.

Abby shook her head. She was still trying to wrap her mind around the idea of asking any guy out. She hadn't even gotten to the *who* part yet.

"Well, don't worry about it. You'll just ask one of Nathan's friends, and then we can all go together!" Chelsea said.

"Nathan's friends? But they're all seventh graders," Abby protested. "I don't know any seventh grade guys."

"That doesn't matter. Ooh, look!" Chelsea had turned her attention back to the Web page. She pointed to a link near the bottom. " 'Sign up to get your daily horoscope sent to you via SMS or e-mail.' That must be new! Should I sign you up, Abby?"

"Sure," Abby said, barely listening. She was still thinking about the dance.

The final bell of the day rang, startling Abby out of her thoughts. "Oh my gosh!" she cried, leaping up from her chair. "I'm going to be late for track."

"Call me later," Chelsea said without looking up.

"I will," Abby told her. And with a swish of her long hair, she hurried out the door.

Abby's feet pounded the cinder track that looped around the practice field behind the school. Her fists pumped at her sides, and her breath whooshed in and out in a steady rhythm.

Abby had always loved to run. At her old school, she'd spent practically every recess organizing races on the playground. When she'd gotten to McKinley, she'd been thrilled to find out there was an actual track team, with daily practices and organized meets.

Abby was mostly a sprinter, but every practice started with a 1.5-mile warm-up, six laps around the track. Most of the kids ran in groups of two or three, talking. But today Abby ran alone. For her, running was the best time to think.

She still couldn't believe that Chelsea was thinking of asking Nathan out. Abby wasn't sure that the two of them had ever even had a conversation, unless you counted playing eyeball hockey in the school hallways. *How does Chelsea even know what he's like?* she wondered.

But it wasn't just that that bothered her — it was the whole boy thing again. Boys were

Chelsea's favorite subject. In fact, they seemed to be the favorite subject of *most* of the girls at McKinley. The girls in Abby's class were always discussing which boys were cutest and who they were crushing on and who they most wanted to date. They played endless games of MASH to find out who they were supposed to marry. Once Abby had even been to a slumber party where the girls practiced kissing on the backs of their hands. It had been totally embarrassing, and Abby had pretended to be asleep until they were done.

Abby liked talking about boys sometimes — there were guys at McKinley she thought were cute — she just didn't want to talk about them *all the time.* Her friends at her old school hadn't been like that. Abby wasn't sure if it was a McKinley thing or if this was just what happened when you got to middle school.

Either way, she sort of missed how things were back in grade school, when guys and girls could just hang out, and it wasn't all about kissing and dating. But she never would have admitted that to Chelsea. Chelsea would have said she was being immature.

As Abby began her sixth lap, her breath came more easily. *Maybe this whole dance thing will just blow over,* she thought. *Tomorrow Chelsea will change her mind. Then we'll all head to the dance together, and it will be a blast, just like before.*

Cheered by this thought, Abby put on a burst of speed. She blazed past the rest of the runners and finished her warm-up in a full-out sprint.

"Whoa! Hang on to some of that steam for the rest of practice," Coach Nelson said as Abby blew past him. Abby slowed to a jog, then trotted back, grinning. She still had plenty of energy left.

"All right, gather up," the coach said as the rest of the team straggled in. "Most of you are going to be working on starts with Amber," he said, nodding at the assistant coach. "But I want all my relay teams down at the south end of the track. We're going to drill handoffs today."

The first track meet of the season was on Friday, so the coaches had started working on techniques they'd need specifically for the meet. Abby would be running the 100-meter dash and 4x100-meter relay. The other girls on Abby's relay team were all older — Suz and Olu were seventh graders, Krista was an eighth grader — and they were the fastest sprinters on the girls' team. Abby was thrilled to be racing with them, but she had been especially proud when the coach made her the anchor. The anchor was the last leg of the relay, and it was the most important position. It showed that the coach had a lot of faith in her.

As they ambled down to the south end of the track, Abby fell into step beside Suz and Olu. "Cam and those girls are talking about renting a limo," Olu was saying. "Like I want to pay for that! David says we can walk to the dance for all he cares. He's so sweet." David was Olu's boyfriend. Abby had never met him, but the way Olu talked about him, he sounded really nice.

Suz turned to Abby, her short dark hair ruffling in the breeze. "Who are you taking to the dance, Rabbit?" she asked. At the start of the track season, Suz and Olu had nicknamed her "Abby Rabbit" because she was small and fast. But before long she'd become just "Rabbit."

"I haven't asked anyone yet," Abby told her.

"Well, you'd better do it soon," Olu advised. "The cute guys always get asked first. You don't want to end up with some bozo just because you waited until the last minute."

"Are you girls planning on gabbing all day, or do you want to do some running?" Coach Nelson asked, coming up behind them. He was wearing his usual black baseball cap, with the brim pulled down low to shade his eyes from the sun.

"Sorry, Coach," they all mumbled, stepping up the pace.

When they got to the far end of the field, Krista was already there, waiting with her hands on her hips. "You guys are pretty slow for sprinters," she snapped. She made it sound like she was talking to all three of them, but she was looking right at Abby.

For some reason, Krista had a grudge against Abby. Suz said it was because last year Krista had been the anchor and she couldn't stand being bumped by a sixth grader. But that didn't make sense to Abby. The year before, Krista had set school records in the Girls 200- and 400-meter dashes, and she'd won first place in the triple long jump at the district meet last year. Abby couldn't touch any of that.

Olu said it was because Krista was worried she wasn't going to be the star anymore. In their timed trial runs, Krista hadn't even come close to her own times from last year. But Abby didn't see what that had to do with her. Aside from the relay, they didn't even compete in the same events.

For the next hour, the relay teams drilled hand-offs. Handing off the baton was the trickiest part of the relay — and it was also the most important.

A fumbled pass could mean the difference between winning and losing a race, and a dropped baton was a disaster. There was no way to recover from a setback like that.

By the time practice was over, Abby was exhausted, not so much from the running, but from the stress of getting the handoff just right. She didn't want to mess up and give Krista a reason to dislike her even more. But Abby thought she'd done pretty well. There had been a few fumbles, but she hadn't dropped the baton once.

As track practice let out, Abby collected her backpack, then walked around to the side of the school to wait for her mom.

"You need a lift, Abby?" asked Olu, who was walking toward a white sedan idling in the school parking lot.

Abby shook her head. "I've got a ride coming. But thanks, anyway."

Before long, the parking lot had cleared out, and Abby was the only one left waiting. Abby wasn't too surprised. Her mom was always running behind.

The afternoon shadows were growing long, and there was a chill in the air. Abby fished a sweatshirt and baseball cap out of her backpack, and pulled them on over her track clothes. She paced up and down the edge of the parking lot, trying to stay warm.

Suddenly, a gust of wind caught the brim of her cap and tugged it off her head.

"Hey!" Abby tried to snatch it, but it soared out of her reach.

As quickly as it had come up, the breeze died down, dropping the hat into a nearby bush. Abby hurried over and fished it out from among the plastic bags and other trash that had been blown there. As she settled the cap on her head, her eyes fell on something stuck between the branches.

"Whoa! Money!" Abby plucked it up and her eyes widened. It was a twenty-dollar bill!

Abby turned, expecting to see someone come chasing after the lost cash. But the parking lot was empty. Across the street, a woman was walking her dog, headed in the opposite direction.

As Abby looked back down at the bill, she suddenly remembered her horoscope. Hadn't it said something about unexpected riches?

"It's just a coincidence," Abby whispered to herself. But her arms prickled with goose bumps.

The honk of a car horn made her jump. Abby

turned and saw a familiar blue Honda pulling into the parking lot. Behind the steering wheel, her mom waved.

Tucking the bill into the pocket of her sweatshirt, Abby ran to meet her mom.

⋆ *Chapter Two* ⋆

The next morning, Abby sat in math class, her chin resting in her hands. Her eyebrows drew together in a frown as she watched her teacher, Ms. Hill, outline a problem on the board.

"Let's say Billy wants a new bike," Ms. Hill told the class, "so he decides to open a lemonade stand. If the bike he wants costs fifty dollars, and Billy sells lemonade for twenty-five cents a cup, how many cups of lemonade will Billy have to sell to get his bike?"

Abby was good at math, but she didn't like story problems. They always left out way too much of the story.

"Marcus," Ms. Hill said to a scrawny kid with an overgrown flattop who was slouched down in his chair, "can you tell us how to solve this problem?"

Marcus remained slumped in his seat, studying the board for a moment. "No offense, Ms. Hill, but what kid would go to all that trouble for a cruddy fifty-dollar bike?"

A few kids snickered, and every eye in the classroom turned to Ms. Hill to see what she would do. Marcus Gruber was always getting in trouble for making smart-aleck comments in class or pulling stupid stunts, like belching the entire national anthem during a school assembly. A lot of the sixth grade guys thought Marcus was hilarious. Most everyone else just thought he was a pain.

Ms. Hill apparently wasn't in a fighting mood. "Interesting observation, Marcus. But how do you know how much work it will be unless we solve the problem?"

Marcus just shrugged and scrunched lower in his seat.

Abby raised her hand. "Yes, Abby?" said Ms. Hill.

"I think Marcus has a point," Abby said.

Everyone, including Marcus, swiveled in their seats to stare at Abby. Even Ms. Hill seemed surprised. "Oh?" she said, her eyebrows arching high on her forehead. "In what way?"

Abby knew she might get in trouble for what she was about to say. But the thing was, Marcus's remark had touched on exactly what was bothering her about the story problem.

"I don't know if you've ever had a lemonade stand, Ms. Hill, but it's not a very good way to make money. Billy would have to sell lemonade all summer, and then he still wouldn't have a very nice bike."

"I see," Ms. Hill said shortly. "So you're saying Billy needs a better way to make money."

Abby nodded.

"He should just ask his parents for the bike!" a kid called out.

Ms. Hill frowned. "Well, Billy would be pretty spoiled then. And we wouldn't have a math problem, would we?"

Abby raised her hand again. "Yes, Abby?" Ms. Hill said.

"Well, maybe Billy could earn *some* of the money," Abby suggested. "And then when his parents saw he was serious, they'd pitch in some money, too. That's what we're doing on the track team. See, all the kids on the team really want to get a new track — one of the good rubber kinds that are easier to run on — but the school doesn't want to pay for it. So we're having a bake sale to earn money for it, and then hopefully the school will put in some money, too."

The kids were really staring at Abby now, and Ms. Hill had an odd expression on her face. Abby wondered if she'd taken it too far. She was glad Chelsea wasn't in her math class. Chelsea would have said Abby was totally geeking out.

"So, um . . . come out and buy a brownie on Monday," she added quickly.

Before Ms. Hill could reply, the bell rang. The classroom filled with the sounds of books slamming and desks scraping as the kids leaped up from their seats.

"Your homework for tonight is on page one twenty-one in your math books," the teacher shouted over the din. "And Abby, would you mind staying after class for a minute?"

Abby got a funny, anxious feeling in her stomach. Ms. Hill had never asked her to stay after class before. *I should have just kept my big mouth shut,* Abby thought.

As the rest of the kids filed out of the classroom, Abby nervously approached her teacher's desk. Ms. Hill was leaning against it, rolling the stick of chalk between her hands. She had a long, narrow face and heavy eyebrows that gave her a rather stern look.

"I guess that story problem was a bit outdated," Ms. Hill said with a little smile.

Abby wasn't sure whether or not to agree, so she decided not to say anything.

Ms. Hill set the chalk down and dusted off her hands. "You know the elections for next year's class officers are coming up. Have you ever considered running?"

"What?" Abby stared at her. This was not the conversation she'd been expecting. "You mean, running for class president?"

"I was thinking treasurer, specifically," said Ms. Hill. "But, of course, you could run for whatever office interested you most."

"Um," said Abby. "I don't know. What would I have to do?"

"We don't allow campaigning at McKinley," Ms. Hill explained. "Candidates are elected based on their speeches alone. So all you'd have to do is sign up — and, of course, come up with a winning speech.

"I'm one of the advisors to the student council," Ms. Hill went on. "And I think you'd make a good class rep. You work hard, you have interesting ideas, and you're not afraid to speak up — those are leadership qualities. I think it could be a really good experience for you."

Abby felt a surge of pride that went all the way down to her toes. "Okay," she said. "I'll give it some thought."

"Do that," Ms. Hill said. "But don't wait too long. Today is the last day to sign up if you want to run. The assembly for election speeches is next week."

Next week! That's so soon! Abby thought. "Thanks for the heads-up, Ms. H."

"See you in class tomorrow, Abby," her teacher replied.

Abby collected her books and headed for the door. She felt like she did when she'd just beat her own best time in a track race.

Should I do it? she asked herself as she walked to her locker. Abby liked the idea of trying something new. But between track and her schoolwork, she already had plenty to keep her busy. Abby wished she had more time to think it over. She wasn't good at making snap decisions.

As she opened her locker door, she noticed the message light on her phone was blinking. *Probably Chelsea, wondering why I'm not at lunch,*

Abby thought. She opened the text message and read:

DAILY HOROSCOPES BY MIZ ASTRID

LIBRA: YOU MAY RECEIVE AN EXCITING NEW OPPORTUNITY TODAY. GO FOR IT! YOU'D BE GREAT FOR THE JOB.

Abby stared at the screen. Where had the message come from? Then she remembered: Chelsea had signed her up to get her daily horoscope sent to her phone.

Abby reread the text, hardly believing her eyes. Here was the answer to the question she'd been asking just seconds before. *Maybe there's more to this horoscope stuff than I thought,* she mused.

Either way, it seemed like a sign. *I am going to go for it!* Abby decided. On her way to the cafeteria, she stopped by the school office and put her name on the list of candidates for seventh grade class treasurer.

In the lunchroom, she spotted Chelsea sitting with their friends Sara and Toshi. As Abby walked up, she overheard Sara saying, "I don't know, I just think it's weird."

"Hey, where've you been?" Chelsea asked as Abby tossed her lunch bag down on the table and slid into an empty seat next to her.

Abby couldn't contain her grin. "Guess what? I'm running for class treasurer."

"Really?" Chelsea's eyebrows drew down in a little frown. "Since when?"

"Since right now." Abby took her sandwich out of her bag and unwrapped it. "After math today Ms. Hill told me I should run. So I thought about it and signed up!"

"Can teachers do that?" asked Sara, looking worried. "You know, make you run for office?"

"She's not *making* me," said Abby. "She just said she thought I'd be good for the job."

"That's Abby, teacher's pet." Chelsea patted Abby's head as if she were a cat.

"I am not teacher's pet," Abby protested. "Anyway, what's wrong with running for class treasurer?"

"Nothing's *wrong* with it. I'm just surprised, that's all," Chelsea said. But her tone implied that it wasn't something *she'd* ever do. Suddenly, Abby felt a pang of uncertainty. *Is running for treasurer uncool?* she wondered. *I probably should have talked it over with Chelsea first.*

"Who else is running?" Toshi asked as she nibbled at a French fry.

"Tyson Storey," Abby said. "And Jennifer Peters, I think."

"Jennifer Peters smells like mothballs," Toshi said. "You'll totally beat her. But Tyson is supercute."

Abby gave her a wounded look. "Are you saying you'd vote for Tyson over me, just because you think he's good-looking?"

"No!" Toshi blinked innocently. "I'll totally vote for you. I'm just saying *other* girls might vote for him."

Chelsea put her arm around Abby's shoulders. "We'll *all* vote for you," she said. "And we'll tell everyone else to vote for you, too."

"Thanks." Abby gave her a grateful smile. She picked up her sandwich again and took a huge bite.

"Speaking of cuties," Chelsea said, turning to Toshi, "I think Dan is perfect for you."

"What are you guys talking about?" Abby mumbled through a mouthful.

"The dance," Toshi explained. "We've all decided who we're asking."

"You've all decided . . . ?" Abby's voice trailed off. So Chelsea hadn't forgotten about the dance after all. And all the other girls were asking guys, too.

"All except for Sara here." Toshi gave Sara a poke.

"I just think it's weird for girls to ask boys out," Sara declared. "Boys are supposed to ask *us* out."

"Uh, hel-*lo*." Toshi snapped her fingers in Sara's face. "Welcome to the twenty-first century. Girls don't sit around waiting for boys to ask them out anymore. And besides, it's a girl-ask-boy dance. So even if a boy wanted to ask you, he couldn't."

"Well, who are *you* going to ask, Abby?" Sara said, turning to her.

Abby could feel her face turn pink as the girls all looked at her. "I'm not really sure yet. . . ."

"Well, you can't wait too long," said Toshi. "Or all the cute boys will be taken."

Did I miss some memo or something? Abby wondered. *That's exactly what Olu said yesterday.*

"What about Josh Carter?" suggested Sara.

"Or Kevin Brown?" said Toshi.

"Ethan Kim?"

"Derek Kolowski?"

"Um," said Abby. How was she supposed to decide?

"I know," Chelsea declared suddenly. "Abby should ask Matt Anderson to the dance."

All the girls turned to look at the table of seventh graders where Matt Anderson was sitting. Matt played on the basketball team, and was definitely considered cool. He had long blond hair that fell into his eyes and always wore shorts, no matter how cold it was outside.

"Matt?" Abby's eyes widened in alarm. "I can't ask him."

"Of course you can. You're both blond — you'll look adorable together. And he's friends with Nathan, so we can double-date. It's perfect!" Chelsea exclaimed.

"Matt is pretty perfect," Toshi sighed.

"But he's a seventh grader!" Abby blurted.

"It's better to go with a seventh grader," Chelsea said matter-of-factly. "Sixth grade boys are way too immature."

Before Abby could reply, a shout went up from the next table over. A group of sixth grade boys were clustered around watching something.

"What's going on?" Sara asked, craning her neck to see.

A boy standing at the edge of the crowd turned to Abby and her friends. "Check this out!" he told them excitedly. "Marcus Gruber is trying to see how many gummy bears he can fit in his mouth at once."

The girls got up to watch. Marcus was standing at the end of the next table, stuffing gummy bears into his mouth as fast as he could.

"... eighteen ... nineteen ... twenty ..." someone counted.

"Go! Go! Go!" the boys chanted.

On the twenty-ninth gummy bear, Marcus paused. His cheeks were stretched to the limit. Multicolored drool oozed from the corners of his mouth and dribbled onto his striped polo.

"He's going to choke," Abby said worriedly.

"He's going to *puke*," said Chelsea.

The crowd held its breath. Finally, Marcus reached in a finger and dislodged a few gummy bears. A second later, the whole gooey mass tumbled out of his mouth. It landed on the table with a sticky splat.

"Eww!" Everyone leaped back. Marcus gave a slobbery laugh and wiped his mouth on the back of his hand.

"Look out," someone murmured. "Jenkins is coming."

All the kids scrambled back to their seats as Ms. Jenkins, the lunchroom monitor, came charging over, her shoes squeak-squeaking on the waxed floor. Ms. Jenkins was built like a pit bull, and she was about as friendly. "What's going on here?" she snapped.

Just then her gaze fell on the mangled gummy bears. She let out a little gasp, and her eyes narrowed into slits. "Who is responsible for this *mess*?" she demanded. She made "mess" sound like "murder."

Everyone fell silent, pretending suddenly to be very focused on eating lunch. Out of the corner of her eye, Abby saw Marcus sidling away, his hands shoved deep in his pockets.

"As I was saying," Chelsea drawled, reaching for her soda, "sixth grade guys are just way too immature."

Later that afternoon, Abby was kneeling in front of her locker, putting her homework into her backpack, when Chelsea came skipping over to her.

"I did it!" she squealed.

Abby stood up. "You did wh — ow!" She rubbed her head where she'd just banged it on the locker shelf. "You did what?" she repeated, her eyes watering.

"I asked Nathan to the dance!" Chelsea looked like she might explode from joy.

Abby forgot about the pain in her head. "For real? And he said yes?"

"Of course he said yes!" Chelsea threw her arms around Abby. "We're going to have so much fun. Me and Nathan and you and Matt!"

"Oh. Um . . ." Abby had thought about it more during class that afternoon, and she'd decided it seemed weird to ask Matt Anderson to the dance. After all, they'd never even spoken to each other. What if she asked him and he laughed in her face? The thought made Abby sick to her stomach.

"What?" Chelsea's smile faded. "You're asking him, right? You said at lunch today that you were going to ask him."

"Actually . . ." Abby hadn't said any such thing. "I'm still sort of deciding," she told Chelsea.

"Listen, Abby," Chelsea said, looking her squarely in the eye. "I really think you should ask Matt, and not just because we'll all have an amazing time. You have to think about your reputation now, too."

"What do you mean?" asked Abby.

"Well, you're running for class treasurer," Chelsea pointed out. "So you need to project a really good image."

Abby blinked, feeling a little hurt. "You don't think I project a good image?"

"Don't get me wrong," Chelsea said quickly, "everyone likes you and thinks you're nice and everything. But they'll respect you even more when they find out you're going to the dance with a popular guy like Matt."

30

Abby thought about that. Chelsea usually knew about these things. And it certainly couldn't hurt to be seen hanging out with a cool seventh grader. "Maybe you're right," she said at last.

"I know I'm right," Chelsea said. "So you'll ask him? Promise?"

Abby nodded. "Okay," she said. "I promise."

★ *Chapter Three* ★

Thursday morning, Abby woke to her father's voice. "Abby, honey, time to get up."

Abby peeled open her eyes and glanced at her clock. 6:45 A.M. Her alarm usually didn't go off until 7:00. She burrowed back down under the covers.

Her dad gave her a gentle shake. "Wake up, Abby. My car won't start, so I'm taking your mom's. You're going to have to take the bus to school today."

Abby's eyes snapped open. She looked at the clock again: 6:46. "Dad," Abby groaned, "the bus comes in less than half an hour. I barely have time to get ready. Can't you take me to school on your way to work?"

"Sorry, Ab. I've got an early meeting this morning, and I'm already running late," her dad said as he headed for the door.

"You could have at least woken me up earlier," Abby grumbled as she threw off the covers and climbed out of bed.

She stumbled across the hall to the bathroom and peered into the mirror. Her eyes were puffy, she had pillow marks on her face, and her hair was Bride-of-Frankenstein messy. She didn't even have time to shower. A wash and blow-dry was out of the question.

Ugh! Abby thought. *Of course this would happen on the day I need to look good.*

She wasted four whole minutes trying to fix her hair with a comb and some water, before finally just pulling it back into a ponytail. She brushed her teeth, splashed cold water on her face, and headed back into her room to get dressed.

"Dress? Skirt? Jeans?" Abby said, whipping through the clothes in her closet. She always had a hard time deciding what to wear, but today especially. Chelsea's comment about needing to project a good image was still ringing in her mind.

Where is my pink baby-doll T-shirt? she wondered. Oh, there it was, crumpled in a pile of dirty laundry with a ketchup stain down the front. Wonderful. Abby finally settled on a green sweater, wide-leg jeans, and a pair of cute brown flats.

In the kitchen, Abby's mother was bent over the cutting board, chopping. The room reeked of onions. "Ugh, Mom. Do you have to do that so early?" Abby complained, her eyes tearing up at the smell.

"I've got a big party tomorrow night," her mom explained. "I just hope your dad's car is working by then." Abby's mom ran a catering business from their home. She was often cooking things like duck canapés and pastry cheese straws at weird times of the day.

Abby plugged her nose and got a cereal bar out of the cupboard. She was just peeling off the wrapper when she noticed the time on the microwave clock.

"Dang! I'm going to miss the bus!" Stuffing the bar in her backpack, she grabbed her jacket and hustled out the door. "Bye, Mom!" she hollered over her shoulder.

Outside, rain slashed down from the sky. By the time she'd reached the end of her driveway, Abby wished she'd chosen something else to wear, but it was too late to go back and change.

Her slippery brown flats slapped her heels as she sprinted through puddles. Abby liked to run, but running in flats with a bag full of homework was a whole different story.

She skidded up to the bus stop, just as the bright yellow school bus was about to close its doors. Abby climbed inside, shaking water from her ponytail. As the bus lurched forward, she had to grab the backs of the seats to keep her balance.

Abby hated riding the bus. She hated its stale smell, which was worse on wet days, with all the windows closed and a bunch of damp kids fogging up the place. Nobody cool rode the bus if they could help it. They got rides from their parents or older brothers and sisters. Or, if they were lucky enough to live close to school, they walked.

Abby made her way down the aisle, until she found an empty seat two-thirds of the way back. She scrunched down in the corner, pulled out the cereal bar and her cell phone, and began to text Chelsea:

what up?

Chelsea's reply came a few seconds later:

nada. r u so excited 2 ask matt???

Abby felt nervous all over again. *I'm just asking him to the dance,* Abby reminded herself. *It doesn't have to be a big deal.*

where r u? Chelsea wrote a second later.

Abby sighed and wrote:

bus : (

The bus lurched to a stop, and Abby glanced up from her phone. Another load of kids was piling on. Abby saw Marcus Gruber striding down the aisle, looking for a seat.

Abby gazed out the window, avoiding eye contact. *Please don't sit next to me,* she thought. *Please don't sit next to me. Please don't sit next to —*

Marcus sat down next to her.

"Hey, Crabby. Nice outfit," he said, eyeing her soaked hair and jeans. "You shower with your clothes on this morning?" Marcus chortled at his own joke.

"Very funny." Abby gave him a cold look and went back to texting Chelsea. She'd gotten as far as i h8 the b when Marcus suddenly snatched the phone out of her hand.

"Marcus!" Abby shrieked. "Give it back!"

"Ooh," he smirked, reading her text. "What does *b* stand for, Abby? Boy? Basketball? Big fat bus driver? Hey, Mr. Lucas, Abby hates you!" he shouted up to the front of the bus.

Mr. Lucas glanced in the rearview mirror and frowned.

"Shut up, Marcus," Abby snapped. "Gimme my phone back." She tried to grab it, but he held it out of her reach.

"Let's see who's in Blabby Abby's phone," Marcus said, going into her contacts. "Avery, Amanda, Cyrus . . . Ooh, do you like Cyrus, Abby? Maybe I should let him know . . ."

"No!" Abby lunged. But Marcus was too quick for her. He threw himself into the empty seat opposite theirs. As Abby went after him, she knocked her backpack from the seat. Books, pencils, and papers spilled across the wet bus floor.

"Gaah!" Abby huffed in frustration. All the kids around them were staring, and Abby felt her cheeks turn red.

She hovered a second, torn between going after Marcus and chasing down her stuff before it rolled away into the sticky corners of the bus. One glance at Marcus — who was intently typing away on her phone — made the decision.

"Give it!" Abby pounced on him. Marcus leaned back against the window, fending Abby off with his dirty sneakers. He continued to work the keypad. Abby tried to reach for her phone, but all she got were muddy footprints on her jacket.

"You! Sit down back there!" Mr. Lucas called. He had spotted Abby in the rearview mirror.

"But he's got my — "

"SIT! DOWN!" the driver roared.

Abby went back to her seat and began to collect her spilled books, which a couple kids in nearby seats had helpfully scooped up for her. She couldn't stop watching Marcus. In a panic, she realized he was probably sending stupid messages to all her friends. Or maybe he was even writing boys and telling them she loved them! The thought made Abby want to scream.

"Just give me my phone back," she pleaded once again. She felt close to tears.

"Geez. Fine." Marcus tossed the phone back at her so unexpectedly that Abby fumbled and almost dropped it.

Marcus snorted. "You catch like a girl."

"Jerk," Abby spat back.

Marcus grinned. Then he opened his mouth and belched the entire verse of "Row, Row, Row Your Boat."

"That's revolting." Abby shuddered and turned back to her phone. At once, she went into "sent messages" and checked to see what he'd written. But the last message was the one she'd sent to Chelsea. She checked all her outgoing calls, but there was nothing there either. She couldn't figure out what Marcus had been doing with her phone.

Finally, Abby went back into "drafts" and found the message she'd started before she'd been so rudely interrupted. Abby switched a few letters and sent Chelsea a message:

i h8 marcus gruber!!!

"What happened to you?" Chelsea asked when Abby stormed up to their lockers twenty minutes later.

"I don't even know where to start," Abby grumbled. She opened her locker and checked her reflection in the mirror on the inside of the door. Her hair had started to dry and was looking very frizzy.

"You look like you got caught in a stampede." Chelsea pulled a comb out of her bag and handed it to Abby. "Is that a *footprint* on your coat?"

Abby examined the tread mark on her sleeve and sighed. "Marcus stole my phone," she explained as she dragged the comb through her hair. "I practically got thrown off the bus trying to get it back. By the way, did you get any weird text messages from me this morning?" She winced as the comb hit a snarl.

Chelsea shook her head. "Just the one about you hating Marcus, which isn't so weird. So . . ." She gave Abby's arm an excited little squeeze. "You got my text about asking Matt today, right?"

Abby sighed and snapped the hair band back over her ponytail. "I don't know, Chelsea. I didn't even get to shower this morning. . . ."

"You can't put it off, Abby, or someone else will ask him." Chelsea pulled a tube of lipstick from her bag and applied it using her own locker mirror.

Abby stared. "When did you start wearing lipstick?"

Chelsea puckered at her reflection and added another coat. "I got this yesterday. It's pretty, right?"

Abby nodded. It *was* pretty. The lipstick was a shimmery coral color that looked nice against Chelsea's olive skin. Still, Abby wasn't used to seeing her friend wearing anything more than lip gloss.

"Here, try it on." Chelsea held out the tube to Abby.

Abby hesitated for half a second. Though her parents had never told her she *couldn't* wear makeup, she had the feeling they wouldn't like her wearing lipstick to school. *Oh, what the heck,* she thought. She took the tube and leaned toward the mirror to put in on.

"That looks great on you!" Chelsea exclaimed.

Abby studied her reflection. Against her pale skin and blond hair, the orangey lipstick seemed extra bright. It made her face look unfamiliar.

"Seriously. You look awesome." Chelsea fluffed Abby's bangs with her fingertips. "Look, there's Matt. You should ask him now."

"Now?" Abby turned and saw Matt down the hall, getting a drink from a water fountain. A jolt of nervousness shot through her.

Just then, she felt her cell phone vibrate in her pocket. Abby pulled it out and read the message:

LIBRA: TAKE A CHANCE ON SOMEONE NEW TODAY. YOU NEVER KNOW, THIS COULD BE THE START OF AN EXCITING NEW RELATIONSHIP.

Abby felt a chill down her spine. "This is just getting weird," she muttered. She showed the message to Chelsea, who squealed with excitement.

"You see?" she told Abby. "It's destiny! Go, go, go!" She gave Abby a little push in Matt's direction.

Abby walked slowly down the hall. Her heart was beating like she'd just run a mile at top speed. When she got to where Matt was standing, Abby pressed her lips together and took a deep breath. "Hey, Matt."

Matt turned from the fountain, wiping his mouth on his sleeve. "Oh, hey, Abby."

He knows my name! Abby thought. *That's a good start.* Encouraged, she gave him a bright smile. "Uh, I was wondering — "

Abby broke off. Matt was staring at her mouth, his eyebrows drawn together in a little frown. "You've got . . ." Matt tapped his front teeth.

"What?" Abby's hand flew to her mouth. Did she have food stuck in her teeth?

"Something orange," Matt said. "Lipstick, maybe."

Horrified, Abby ran her tongue over her teeth. "Is it gone now?"

Matt shook his head. "It's kind of a big smear."

Abby scrubbed her front teeth with her index finger. "Dude," said Matt, "you've almost got it. Just a little to the left."

Abby rubbed harder. *Please let a comet fall on the school and strike me dead right now,* she pleaded.

No comet appeared, but a few seconds later the bell for class rang. "I gotta bolt. See you around, right?" Matt said.

He sauntered off down the hall, his books held loosely under one arm. Abby slumped against the wall and covered her burning face with her hands.

"So?" Chelsea came scurrying over. "What did he say?"

Abby peeked at Chelsea between her fingers. "He said, 'You have lipstick on your teeth.'"

"Ooh." Chelsea winced sympathetically. She pulled a tissue from a pack in her purse and handed it to her friend. "So I take it you didn't ask him to the dance?"

"I didn't get around to it." Abby rubbed her

teeth, then wiped the rest of the lipstick off her lips. "I was sort of distracted by the utter humiliation I was feeling."

"Don't worry," said Chelsea. "You'll get another chance."

Abby sighed. *You mean I'm going to have to go through that again?* she thought. This dance business was even harder than she'd thought it would be.

Despite what Chelsea had said, Abby didn't get another chance to ask Matt that day. Once, right before sixth period, she worked up the nerve to walk past his locker, but when she saw him talking to a bunch of other seventh grade guys, she walked right past. And after school, she had to hurry to get to track practice. She didn't want to be late two days in a row.

When she got home that night, there was a message from Chelsea on her phone:

matt's #: 385-5621. call him 2nite!

Abby put the number into her phone, but she didn't call him right away. First she did her homework, then she ate dinner with her parents, then she helped clean up the kitchen, washing and drying each dish thoroughly.

Finally, she went into her room and closed the door. She picked up her phone and reread her horoscope for the day. "'The start of an exciting new relationship,' huh?" Abby murmured to herself. It all seemed a little crazy. But then again, her horoscope hadn't been wrong yet.

Taking a deep breath, she dialed Matt's number. But before it rang, she hung up. She set the phone down, her heart thudding in her chest. *There's got to be an easier way to do this,* she thought.

Abby picked up the phone again and typed out a text message:

will u go 2 the dance with me? abby w.

She read it over and decided it was perfect. This way, she wasn't putting Matt on the spot. He could think it over, and if he didn't want to go, he didn't have to say so to Abby's face. He could write back "no" or "sorry, can't make it" or whatever, and it would be no big deal. They could just ignore each other at school and pretend like it never happened.

Abby took a deep breath, closed her eyes, and pressed SEND.

MESSAGE SENT blipped up on the screen. Abby exhaled. Mission accomplished.

"That wasn't so bad," she said to herself. She brushed her teeth, put on her pajamas, and got into bed, feeling better than she had all day. The ball was in Matt's court now. By tomorrow morning, she'd know the score.

★ Chapter Four ★

Abby slumped in the passenger seat of her mom's car, checking her messages for the twentieth time that morning.

"So it turned out your father's car was just out of gas again," her mom was saying, as she piloted the car down the tree-lined streets toward Abby's school. "I swear I'm going to have to start sticking Post-it notes on that man's forehead so he'll remember to fill up the tank."

"Mmm," said Abby, barely listening. Her stomach felt like it was twisted in knots. She couldn't believe Matt hadn't replied to her text yet.

Abby's mom glanced over at her and sighed. "I wish you would put that thing away, hon. You're going to be at school in just a few minutes. can talk to your friends when you get there

"I was just waiting for a message," Abby said. But she slipped her phone into her backpack.

"You know, when I was your age, people actually had real conversations, with words and everything," her mom said as she pulled up in front of the school.

"I know," Abby replied, opening her door, "but that was back in the dinosaur days, when people lived in caves and there was nothing to do but sit around the campfire and talk."

Her mom rolled her eyes. "Dinosaur days? What are they teaching you at that school?"

"How to live in the twenty-first century," said Abby. She leaned over and gave her mom a kiss on the cheek. "Bye, Mom."

"Have a good day, hon," her mom said as Abby slid out of the car and shut the door.

Inside the school, Abby hurried through the crowded hallway. She was relieved to see Chelsea standing at their lockers.

"He didn't write me back!" were the first words out of Abby's mouth.

"Who didn't write you back?" Chelsea asked.

"Matt! I sent him a text asking him to the dance, and he hasn't replied."

"Well, maybe he just hasn't gotten the message yet," Chelsea said with a shrug.

Abby gave her a doubtful look. "I sent it last night. Oh, I knew this was a bad idea!" she groaned. "He's probably laughing about it with all his friends right now."

Chelsea placed her hands on Abby's shoulders. "Don't freak out," she commanded. "He probably just wants to tell you in person. I'll bet if you catch him in the hall, he'll be like, 'Oh hey, got your message. Of course I want to go to the dance with you.'"

Abby's forehead wrinkled. "You think?"

"Absolutely," said Chelsea.

"Okay." Abby nodded. "So, I'm just going to go over to him and say, 'Hey, Matt. What's up?'"

"You got it," Chelsea told her. "Now, go get him."

Abby took a deep breath, threw her shoulders back, and started toward Matt's locker. But she'd only gone about four steps, when Marcus Gruber blocked her path. He was grinning so widely that Abby could see the metal band of his retainer stretching all the way across his teeth.

Abby tried to step around him, but Marcus wouldn't budge. "So . . . uh, yeah," he said.

"Yeah what?" asked Abby.

Marcus smirked. "*You* know."

This must be some stupid Marcus joke, A

thought with a sigh. She decided she'd get rid of him quicker if she just played along. "Oh yeah. That."

Marcus raised his eyebrows. "So we're cool?"

"You bet," said Abby.

"Okay." Marcus didn't move.

Abby looked over his shoulder. She could see Matt coming down the hall, and he was alone. Now was her chance. "Excuse me, Marcus," she said, "I've got to talk to someone."

"Sure." Marcus stepped aside and let Abby pass. "See you around!" he called after her.

"That was weird," Abby mumbled to herself. But she immediately put Marcus out of her mind. She had bigger things to think about — or make that taller, blonder things. Namely Matt, who was suddenly right in front of her.

"Hi, Matt," she said casually.

"Hey, Abby." Matt tipped his head back, peering at her from beneath his sheepdog-like bangs. "What's up?"

What's up? Abby thought. *That's supposed to be my line! You tell me what's up, Matt Anderson! How come you haven't written me back?*

When Abby didn't reply, Matt gave a slow nod. "Well," he said, "see ya around." He ambled off down the hall.

Abby watched him go, feeling a mixture of

anger, confusion, and total humiliation. How could he not even mention her text?

She stood there until the second bell rang. Then she put her head down and hurried on to class.

By fourth period, Abby still hadn't heard anything from Matt, and she was starting to get really worried. As Ms. Hill outlined another story problem on the board, Abby barely heard a word she said. She was too busy working out her own problem.

Is Matt a jerk, or just totally clueless? she wondered. Before today she hadn't really even wanted to go to the dance with him. But now she couldn't think about anything else!

Abby felt a poke in her ribs. She turned and saw the girl behind her slipping her a note. Her name was written on the front. Abby recognized Sara's round handwriting.

She glanced up at Ms. Hill. The teacher had her back turned, writing on the board. Abby unfolded the note in her lap. It read:

Hey, girl —

What is up? Did you seriously ask Marcus Goober to the dance?

W/B

Sara

Huh? Abby thought. Where had Sara gotten a ridiculous idea like that? **Are you JOKING? No way!** she wrote back. **Who told you that?** She folded the note and passed it to the girl behind her, who passed it on.

As Abby waited for Sara's response, she glared at the back of Marcus's head. *Was that stupid conversation this morning a trick?* she wondered. Had Marcus been trying to make it look as if they were talking so people would think she was asking him to the dance? It was a lame stunt, even for Marcus. When people found out the truth, he would look pretty desperate.

When Sara's note came back, Abby practically tore it open.

Marcus said he had a text from you. He was showing some guys in my last class. He must have made it up and sent it to himself. What a loser!

Abby reread the note three times, feeling ice in the pit of her stomach. It was too much of a coincidence that Marcus had come up with the idea of *pretending* that Abby had sent him a text — when Abby actually *had* sent a text to Matt.

Could Matt have forwarded the message to Marcus? she wondered. *But why would he do that?*

As far as she knew, Matt and Marcus didn't even know each other. They didn't hang with the same crowd, that was for sure.

Either way, she could prove it wasn't true. All she had to do was find the message she'd sent to Matt. She just hoped it was still saved in her phone.

The rest of math crawled by. When the bell finally rang, Abby bolted from her seat, not even bothering to wait for Sara. She sprinted back to her locker, dug her cell phone out of her backpack, and scrolled through her messages until she found the one she'd sent to Matt.

Except she hadn't actually sent it to Matt. At the top of the message in bright red letters it read:

to: marcus rules!

Marcus Rules? How had *that* name gotten into her phone? She checked her contacts. Sure enough MARCUS RULES! was listed right above MATT.

Just then, Abby noticed she had a new message. She eagerly opened it, hoping it might explain what was going on. The message read:

DAILY HOROSCOPES BY MIZ ASTRID

LIBRA: BEWARE DISTRACTIONS AND DOUBLE-CHECK EVERYTHING

"No kidding, Miz Astrid," Abby snapped. "You might have mentioned that a little sooner."

"Who are you talking to?" asked Chelsea, walking up.

"Chelsea!" Abby turned to her friend. "Oh my gosh, I really messed up!"

Chelsea gasped. "What's wrong?"

"I accidentally asked Marcus Gruber to the dance."

"You *what*?" Chelsea started to laugh.

"It's not funny! I meant to send a text to Matt, but I must have hit the wrong name." Abby held out the phone to show her friend.

Chelsea scanned the message, then handed the phone back, holding it between two fingers as if it might have cooties. "Well, that explains why Matt never wrote you back. What's Marcus Goober's number doing in your phone in the first place?" she asked.

Abby sighed. "He must have put it in there when he stole my phone on the bus. What am I going to do?"

"What do you mean what are you going to do? Obviously you can't go to the dance with Marcus.

Just tell him it's a big mistake. It's his fault for messing with your phone in the first place."

"That's true!" Abby suddenly felt indignant. If Marcus hadn't been acting like such a goober on the bus, none of this ever would have happened!

"I'll tell him this afternoon," she said. She gave a little laugh and shrugged her shoulders. "He probably doesn't even want to go to the dance, anyway."

But Abby never found the right moment to tell Marcus that afternoon, and by the end of the day she had other things to worry about. The first track meet of the season was right after school, and all her nerves were jangling. She'd deal with Marcus later, she decided. Right now the race needed her full attention.

Abby stood on the side of the field behind Eastlake Middle School. She grabbed her ankle in one hand, pulling her leg back in a thigh stretch. Out on the track, the second heat of the Girls 800-meter race was just getting started. In the center of the field, boys and girls were competing in the high jump and pole vault.

The afternoon was cool, and although Abby had on a heavy sweatshirt over her track uniform, her legs were pimpled with goose bumps. She did a few jumping jacks to get her blood moving. This was one thing Abby hadn't expected about track meets — all the standing around. She'd already run the 100-meter dash and had come in first in her heat. But that had been more than a half hour ago. Abby had a long wait between her two races, enough time to get cold — and bored.

She closed her eyes and tried to focus on the relay ahead of her. She imagined the baton passing smoothly from Suz's hands to hers, over and over again. "Just like we did on Tuesday," Abby whispered to herself.

Abby felt a rough tap on her shoulder, and her eyes flew open. Olu was standing in front of her. "What are you doing?" she asked.

"Just getting psyched for the race," Abby told her.

"Well, I hope it worked, 'cause we're up," said Olu.

"Now?" How had that happened? Abby had thought she still had ages until the relay started. She hadn't even finished warming up!

She kneeled down to tie her shoelaces in her lucky backward double knot. Abby had just finished with her left shoe, when she heard someone call her name.

She looked up into the bleachers and saw Marcus Gruber giving her the thumbs-up. "Get 'er done, Waterman!" he shouted.

What is he *doing here?* Abby thought, as the Spring Dance mess flooded back into her mind. She shook her head in frustration. Marcus was the last thing she wanted to be thinking about right now.

"Come on, Rabbit! Hurry up." Suz waved at her impatiently. Krista and Olu were already trotting out onto the track. Abby quickly tied her right shoe and hurried after them.

The girls got into position in their lanes. Abby was lined up next to a girl from Eastlake, who was at least a head taller than Abby. She tried to ignore this Amazon and kept her eyes trained straight ahead.

The crack of the starter pistol sent a rush of adrenaline through Abby's veins. She looked over to see Krista flying down the track, a whole stride ahead of the rest of the girls. Just before Krista reached her, Olu started to run. A second later the baton was in Olu's hand, and she was tearing down the track toward Suz, her tiny braids streaming out behind her. When she reached Suz, the baton passed smoothly from hand to hand again. They were in the lead!

This is it! Abby thought. When Suz was only a few paces away, Abby started to accelerate, holding her hand back for the baton. As soon as it was in her grasp, she shifted into gear. They had it! They were going to win! They —

It happened so fast Abby didn't know what had hit her. One second, she was racing toward the finish line, and in the next instant her feet had gone out from under her. She hit the ground hard, the baton rolling away from her hand.

After that, everything seemed to go in slow motion: the other runners' feet pounding past her as they sprinted toward the finish line, the groans of dismay from the crowd, the horrified looks on her teammates' faces. . . .

Abby tried to pick herself up, but the fall had knocked the wind out of her. Her right knee was on fire, and Abby realized it must have struck the ground first. A moment later, a referee was hovering over her, asking her if she could stand.

Abby nodded, tears pricking her eyes. Her palms stung from where they'd smacked the ground. As the ref helped her up, she could see the Amazon from Eastlake at the finish line. Her fists were raised triumphantly in the air.

Abby limped over to the side of the track, where Krista, Olu, and Suz were all waiting. Krista's arms were folded across her chest and her jaw jutted out in an angry way.

"Rabbit, are you okay?"

"What happened out there?"

Suz and Olu fluttered around her, their expressions switching back and forth between concern and frustration. Abby could tell they were disappointed, but trying not to show it.

"I know what happened out there," Krista said coldly. "Take a look at Abby's shoes."

Abby looked down, and her heart sank. Her right shoe was untied, the laces flopping around like flabby noodles.

"That's what we get for having a sixth grader in our relay," Krista sneered. "She's so pathetic she can't even tie her own shoes."

Abby looked to Suz and Olu. But for once they didn't tell her to ignore Krista.

"You tripped over your *shoelaces*?" Suz snapped. "Geez, Abby, get it together!"

And without another word, Abby's three teammates turned and walked away.

★ Chapter Five ★

"Come out, Abby!" Chelsea trilled.

"I don't want to," Abby grumbled from behind the dressing room door.

"You have to show me." Chelsea's voice was stern. "We promised we'd show each other everything."

You mean you *promised,* Abby thought with a sigh. It was Saturday afternoon, and the two friends were shopping at Evening Rose, an upscale boutique in the mall. Chelsea had called first thing that morning to say they needed to find dresses for the dance.

Abby's plan had been to stay home in her pajamas, watching cartoons and moping about the track meet. But her parents had insisted that she go. "You need to get out of the house and have fun," they'd said.

So far, Abby was not having fun. Chelsea had insisted that Evening Rose was the best place to find dresses, but everything there was super-expensive. Abby had felt out of place from the moment they walked in.

"Abby," Chelsea called. "I'm waiting."

Abby gritted her teeth and stepped out from behind the curtain. "Ooh!" Chelsea squealed, clasping her hands together. "You look gorgeous!"

Abby looked down at the floor-length turquoise dress she was wearing. It was the smallest size they had, but the top was baggy, and the skirt was so long it puddled around Abby's ankles. She felt like a little kid playing dress up. "I look totally lame," she told Chelsea. "This dress is way too big for me."

"Dresses always have to be taken in," Chelsea said with a wave of her hand. "Let's try it with your hair down." She loosened Abby's ponytail and fanned her long hair out over her shoulders. "Take a look."

Abby took a step toward the mirror and promptly tripped over the hem. "Oh, perfect," she snapped. "I can wear this to the dance and do *another* face-plant in front of everyone."

Chelsea heaved an impatient sigh. "Will you stop sulking about that?" she said. "It was just one race."

"Just one race? Chelsea, I tripped over my *shoelaces*. Do you have any idea how lame that is? I let the whole team down!" Abby still couldn't think about it without cringing.

"They'll get over it," Chelsea said lightly. "And in the meantime, *you* need to get over it, because we have shopping to do. So, what do you think of my dress?" Chelsea did a little fashion model spin. She was wearing a short black sequined dress with spaghetti straps and a big bow around the waist.

"Don't you think it's a little fancy?" Abby asked.

"This is our first big dance," Chelsea replied, turning to admire herself in the three-way mirror. "We have to look totally glamorous."

"Glamorous?" Abby wrinkled her nose. "We're going to a dance in the cafeteria, Chels, not the Academy Awards."

"You are so grumpy today," Chelsea complained, without turning her eyes from the mirror. "I think this dress looks nice."

"It looks nice on her, too," Abby pointed out. At the other end of the dressing room, a very tan older woman with short, frosted hair was looking at herself in another three-way mirror. She had on the same dress as Chelsea.

"Hmph." Chelsea frowned. But Abby knew she'd gotten through.

"Why don't we go look at Blue Beat?" Abby suggested, mentioning one of Chelsea's favorite stores. "They'll probably have something dance-worthy there."

Chelsea turned to her and smiled. "Abby, that's the first good idea you've had all day."

In Blue Beat, pop music was blaring, and the store was packed with middle school and high school kids. As Chelsea charged around, grabbing dresses off the racks, Abby trailed behind, her mind still on the track meet.

Krista, Olu, and Suz had barely spoken to her on the bus ride back to school. Even Coach Nelson had seemed annoyed. All he'd said was, "Double knot your laces next time," but Abby could tell from his tone that he was disappointed.

The thing is, I always *double knot,* Abby thought, going over it in her mind for the hundredth time. But she'd let herself get distracted, and she'd paid the price. It had all played out just as her horo-scope had said it would. If only she'd paid more attention!

Well, she wasn't taking any more chances. From now on, she was going to do *exactly* what her horoscope said. Abby pulled out her phone and reread the message she'd received that morning:

DAILY HOROSCOPES BY MIZ ASTRID

LIBRA: YOU MAY FIND YOURSELF WITH A DIFFICULT CHOICE TO MAKE. LUCKILY, YOU DON'T HAVE TO LOOK FAR FOR THE ANSWER. IT WILL BE CLEAR IN YOUR HEART.

The message struck Abby as particularly omi-nous. *What difficult choice?* she wondered. She hoped it wasn't anything more serious than which dress to buy. After everything that had happened in the last couple of days, she wasn't sure she was up to dealing with more than that.

Chelsea walked up, her arms loaded with clothes. "I'm going to try this stuff on. Haven't you found anything yet?"

Abby glanced around. She'd been so busy thinking that she'd forgotten what they were there to do. "I haven't finished looking," she told Chelsea.

"Well, hurry up. I'll meet you in there," Chelsea said as she headed off to the dressing room.

Abby listlessly poked through the racks. Usually she loved shopping with Chelsea, but today her heart just wasn't in it.

She was about to give up, when she spotted a dress hanging on a rack at the back of the store. It was Abby's favorite shade of cornflower blue, and had a scooped neck and a pleated, drop-waist skirt.

In the dressing room, Abby discovered that it fit perfectly. The dress brought out the color of her eyes, and the drop waist gave it a fun, flapperish quality that Abby liked. She checked the price tag and saw it was on sale — fifty percent off!

Sold! Abby thought, turning this way and that in front of the mirror. *If this is my "difficult choice," then the rest of the day should be a breeze!*

Just then, Chelsea stepped out of her dressing room. She had on an emerald-green wrap dress with pretty gold trim. "There you are!" she said when she saw Abby. "I was wondering when you were going to get here. What do you think?" She smoothed the skirt and struck a pose.

"Nice." Abby nodded. *Way better than the black sequins,* she added to herself.

"I think I'm going to get it," Chelsea said. "What about you? Haven't you found anything?"

"Yeah!" Abby smiled and did a little spin. "It's cute, right?"

"For the *dance*?" Chelsea wrinkled her nose. "Abby, be serious. That dress is made out of T-shirt material."

"Oh." Abby's face fell. She hadn't noticed what material it was made out of. She'd just thought the dress was pretty.

"Don't worry," Chelsea said, misunderstanding the look on Abby's face. "I know shopping isn't your biggest talent. But now that I've found my dress, I can help you. We'll find something really good."

Abby turned back to the mirror again. She really loved the blue dress. *But Chelsea knows what she's talking about,* Abby reminded herself. She wouldn't get the blue dress now. Together, she and Chelsea would find something else for her to wear to the dance.

"So where to next?" Chelsea asked, swinging her bag from Blue Beat. The green dress was folded inside, wrapped in layers of pink tissue paper.

"I don't know about you, but I could really go

for a frozen lemonade," Abby said. "All this shopping is making me thirsty."

"Me too!" said Chelsea. "Frozen lemonade first — and *then* we'll find you the perfect dress."

They were almost to the food court, when Chelsea suddenly stopped in her tracks and grabbed Abby's arm. "Omigosh!" she gasped. "It's Nathan and Matt!"

Abby followed her gaze. The two boys were across the mall, about to head into a big electronics store.

Abby's first impulse was to hide. *Relax,* she told herself. *They're just guys.* Besides, hiding was now out of the question. Chelsea was already flailing an arm as if she was trying to flag down a helicopter. "Hey, Nathan!" she shouted across the mall.

The boys looked up, and Nathan raised a hand. "What up, Rinaldi?" he hollered back.

Chelsea giggled. "This is so great," she said, dragging Abby along.

"Hi, you two," Chelsea said flirtatiously when they met up with the boys.

"Hey," Matt said, flipping his hair out of his eyes.

"Hey," said Abby.

"So what are you guys up to?" Chelsea asked brightly.

"Not much," Nathan said. "We were just headed to ElectroMania to try out the new Wii game."

"Really?" Chelsea couldn't have looked more impressed if Nathan had said he was heading to NASA to test out the new space shuttle. "I have *totally* been wanting to check that out."

Abby raised her eyebrows and gave her an excuse-me-but-since-when-are-you-into-video-games look. Chelsea ignored her.

"You want to come with us?" Nathan asked with a shrug.

"Actually, we were just on our way to get something to dr — ouch!" Abby yelped as Chelsea dug her elbow into Abby's ribs.

"We can do that *later,* Abby," Chelsea muttered through clenched teeth. She turned to Nathan and flashed her dimples. "Let's go!"

"I really am thirsty, you know," Abby grumbled as they followed the boys into the electronics store.

"Abby, what is your problem?" Chelsea hissed into her ear. "This is your perfect chance to ask Matt to the dance!"

"Right." Abby sighed. Considering how many times she'd already tried to ask Matt to the dance, it was hard to believe she still hadn't done it yet.

ElectroMania was packed with Saturday shoppers. From the yellow banners everywhere, Abby guessed they were having a sale. The new Wii game turned out to be an off-road driving course. As Nathan grabbed a control stick, Chelsea shoved her shopping bag into Abby's hands and jumped in next to him, leaving Abby alone with Matt.

Abby fiddled with her hair, trying to think of something to say. "So, you play a lot of games?" she asked Matt.

"Yeah, I guess so," said Matt with a little shrug.

"Do you have a Wii at home?" Abby tried again.

"Yeah." Matt's eyes were glued to the screen, where Nathan's car was tearing across a sand dune. Chelsea's car skidded along behind it, spraying sand from its tires.

"So, I guess the basketball team is having a pretty good season? You must be psyched," Abby said to Matt.

"Yeah."

Abby's brow furrowed. *Does he ever say anything other than "yeah"?* she wondered.

A peal of laughter rang through the air. Abby looked over in time to see Chelsea's car narrowly avoid hitting a cactus.

"You stink at this game," Nathan told her.

"No way! I'm on you like glue," Chelsea shot back, sending her car tearing after Nathan's.

Abby sighed. She had the feeling that Nathan and Chelsea were going to be there for a while. "I think I'm just going to look around," she told Matt. He barely nodded, still watching the game.

Abby wandered off with no real direction. Electronics stores didn't really interest her. She liked watching TV as much as anyone else, but whenever anyone started talking plasma versus LCD her eyes tended to glaze over.

Abby walked up and down the aisles until she came to a rack of sale DVDs. She stopped and began to flip through the cases. Most of them were action flicks, but there were a few comedies mixed in, too.

She was just reaching for a romantic comedy called *The Kiss List* when she bumped into someone grabbing for the same case.

"Sorry," Abby mumbled, glancing up. "Marcus!"

"Abby!" Marcus withdrew his hand so quickly that he knocked the movie from the rack. It went flying to the floor.

Abby picked it up. "Have you seen this?" she asked in surprise. She hadn't pegged Marcus as the kind of guy who'd like romantic comedies.

"Yeah . . . I mean, *no*," Marcus said quickly. "That is, my sister was watching it, so I might have caught some of it . . . you know, just in passing." Was it Abby's imagination, or was he blushing a little? "What are you doing here?" he asked, changing the subject.

"Just wandering around," Abby said with a shrug. "I'm here with Chelsea, but she's over playing video games."

Marcus raised his eyebrows. "I didn't know Chelsea was a gamer."

"Neither did I," Abby said drily.

"So, um . . . nice going in the track meet yesterday," Marcus said.

Abby's jaw clenched. Of course, she should have known that Marcus would seize the opportunity to make fun of her. *He's such a jerk,* she thought. "What were *you* doing there?" she snapped. "Eastlake is all the way across town."

Marcus blinked. "My dad lives over by Eastlake," he explained. "I was at his house after school and decided to go by the meet. I heard you took second place in the 100-meter dash."

Was this just the warm-up to his joke? Abby wondered. Well, she'd beat him to the punch line. "Yeah, it was real great," she said bitterly. "Until I fell on my face."

Marcus winced. "Yeah, I saw that. It looked like it hurt."

Abby couldn't believe it. Wasn't he going to say anything sarcastic about her tripping over her own shoelaces? "I think I set the record for stupid-est sports moment ever," she told Marcus. She knew she should just drop it. But self-pity had started to bubble up in her, and she couldn't stop herself.

"Aw, that's nothing," said Marcus. "When I played club soccer last fall, I stopped the ball with my face so many times, the coach started to worry I was going to get brain damage."

Abby couldn't help herself. She laughed. "Really? Were you the goalie or something?"

"Nah, I just have this really magnetic face," Marcus told her. He raised his eyebrows and added, "You should see what happens when I go bowling."

Abby imagined Marcus with a bowling ball stuck to his face, and started to giggle harder. "Is this supposed to make me feel better?" she asked.

Marcus shrugged. "I don't know. So, what's in the bag?" he asked, nodding at the Blue Beat bag that Abby was still holding.

"It's Chelsea's," Abby said. Suddenly, she remembered why they were at the mall in the first place and her laughter dried up. She needed to tell Marcus that she hadn't meant to ask him to the dance. And now was as good a time as any.

Abby licked her lips, suddenly feeling nervous. "Hey, um, you know how you stole my phone on the bus the other day?" she asked.

"Yeah." Marcus looked sheepish. "Are you still mad about that? Because I thought —"

"Marcus," a voice interrupted. A tall girl with curly brown hair came striding over to them. "We're about ready to go. Are you almost done? Oh hey," she said, noticing Abby.

The girl had the same square face and freckles as Marcus, but she was older. Maybe fifteen or sixteen, Abby thought. She had a wide, friendly smile. "Introduce your friend," she said, nudging Marcus.

Marcus rolled his eyes. "Abby, this is my sister, Trish. Trish, meet Abby."

Trish's mouth drew into a little round O. "You're Abby? You mean, *the* Abby. The Abby that Marcus is going to the Spring Dance with?"

"Um . . ." said Abby.

"Trish, shut up. It's no big deal," Marcus growled.

"No big deal? Don't let him fool you," Trish told Abby, wrapping her arm around her brother's neck in a cross between a stranglehold and a hug. "He's totally stoked. You should have seen him the night you asked him. Of course, he wouldn't tell me who it was at first. I had to hang him by his ankles until he confessed."

"Trish!" Marcus cried, trying to twist out of her grip. He had turned red all the way to the tips of his ears.

"All right, charmer," Trish said, releasing him. She turned to Abby and held out her hand. "Abby, a pleasure to meet you. Marcus, we'll be waiting for you outside." She gave him an elaborate wink, then turned and walked away.

Marcus stared daggers at her back. "My sister is crazy," he told Abby. "Don't pay any attention to her."

"Mmm." Abby was barely listening. She was still thinking about what Trish had said. Marcus was *stoked* to go to the dance?

"So what did you want to tell me about your phone?" Marcus asked.

"It's kind of funny. . . ." Abby stalled. The gears of her mind were still turning. *I never meant to ask Marcus to the dance — AND he messed with my phone — so I don't owe him anything,* she reminded herself.

It all made sense. So what was stopping her?

Marcus was looking at her, waiting for her answer. Abby laughed weakly and held up her phone. "The phone is fine. I mean, it's working and everything."

"Well, it should be working," he replied with a confused frown. "It's not like I puked on it or something."

"What did Marcus puke on now?" Chelsea asked, coming up and putting her arm around Abby's shoulders. "Abby, where have you been? I've been looking all over for you."

"I've been right here," Abby told her. "I ran into Marcus."

"Hey," Marcus said.

Chelsea barely glanced at him. "Come on," she said to Abby. "Nathan and Matt are waiting for us outside."

"Okay." Abby nodded, relieved to have an excuse to leave. "Well, see you around, Marcus."

"Later, gator," said Marcus.

"Ugh, poor you," Chelsea whispered to Abby as they walked toward the door. "Stuck talking to Marcus Goober. Was he being revolting?"

"Actually, he was weirdly normal," Abby said, glancing back over her shoulder at him.

"He must have been having an off day," Chelsea said, steering them toward the food court. "Abby, you are so going to love me. I took care of everything!"

"What do you mean?" Abby asked.

"You'll see," Chelsea said, her eyes twinkling.

Nathan and Matt were sitting at a yellow table in front of King Dog. They each had supersize Cokes and a pile of straws and were blowing the paper covers off the straws at each other.

"I found Abby," Chelsea said as she slid into the seat next to Nathan. She giggled as he fired a straw cover at her. Abby sat down next to Matt. She wondered if he'd shoot a straw cover at her, but he was busy peeling the plastic lid off his soda. He took a huge gulp of Coke, then turned to Abby. "Yeah, I'll go to the dance with you."

Abby stared at him, too stunned to answer.

"I told Matt that you've been dying to ask him, but you're too shy," Chelsea piped up from across the table. She leaned over and took a sip from

Nathan's Coke. "You want to go to the dance with Matt, right, Abby?"

Abby opened her mouth, but no words came out. She couldn't go to the dance with Matt because she was still going with Marcus. *But who in their right mind would pick Marcus over Matt?* she thought.

Just then her gaze fell on a bunch of balloons bobbing near the entrance to a greeting card store. A large heart-shaped balloon floated above the others. Emblazoned in the middle in bright pink letters were the words SAY YES!

Abby's horoscope flashed through her mind: *The answer will be clear in your heart.*

"Yes," Abby murmured, her eyes still fixed on the heart-shaped balloon.

"Great!" Chelsea said. "Then it's all settled." She leaned over to Matt and added, "Abby's so shy, sometimes she just needs a little push."

Normally, Abby would have been annoyed that Chelsea was talking about her like she wasn't even there. But she was too confused by what had just happened. She hadn't even wanted one date for the dance — and now she had two!

⋆ *Chapter Six* ⋆

By Sunday morning, Abby still hadn't come up with a solution to her problem. As she sat at the breakfast table with her parents, eating a bagel with cream cheese, she mulled things over in her mind.

Of course I should go to the dance with Matt, she thought. *He's cute and popular and cool. Plus, he's a seventh grader, and he's best buds with Chelsea's date.* Abby counted on her fingers. That was five reasons right there.

What was more, her horoscope had been hinting all week that she should go with Matt. Hadn't it said she would start an "exciting new relationship" the day she'd decided to ask him? And yesterday, when she hadn't known what to do, her horoscope had said the answer would be in her heart — and then, plain as day, she'd seen a heart with the answer in it! Granted, it hadn't been *her* heart exactly. But Abby wasn't going to get picky about details.

Marcus, on the other hand — well, Abby could only come up with reasons why she *shouldn't* go to the dance with Marcus. He was loud. He was obnoxious. He wasn't afraid to drool in public. He actually considered burping to be a form of communication. When it came down to it, Marcus lived up to his nickname — he was just a big goober.

The problem is, Abby thought with a sigh, *un-asking Marcus is turning out to be a lot harder than I thought it would be.* So what was she supposed to do? Abby didn't like making decisions — and this one was a doozy.

"What's on your mind, Abs?" her dad asked as he refilled his cup of coffee. "You've hardly said a word all morning."

"Are you still upset about the track meet?" her mom asked. "It doesn't help to dwell on these things, sweetheart. You'll do better next time, I know you will."

"It's not that . . ." Abby said. Could her parents tell her what do to about the dance? she wondered. Maybe it was worth a try.

"Did you ever ask someone to a dance?" she asked.

"Sure, lots of times," said her dad. "I asked your mother to a dance once, and she turned me down."

"In high school?" Abby's parents had been high school sweethearts. Abby knew lots of stories about them, but she'd never heard this one.

Her dad nodded. "She broke my heart."

Abby's mom rolled her eyes. "Hardly. As I recall, you turned right around and asked Sheila Briggs to the dance. Sheila was a cheerleader," she added for Abby's benefit.

"And she was also a huge bore. Worst dance I ever went to." Mr. Waterman refilled his wife's coffee cup, then kissed the top of her head. Abby's mom smiled.

"Why did you turn Dad down?" Abby asked her mom. "Didn't you like him?"

"Actually, I had a big crush on him. But I already had a date to the dance," her mom explained. "Backing out to go with someone else seemed like a pretty crummy thing to do."

"Oh," Abby said. That wasn't what she'd been hoping to hear. She took a small sip of orange juice. "But, um . . . what if your first date didn't really mean to ask you? Would you still have wanted to go with him?"

Both her parents looked at her. "I'm not sure I follow you," her mom said.

"Well," Abby looked down at the table, carefully folding and unfolding her napkin, "for example, what if he meant to ask someone else, but accidentally asked you instead?"

Her mom laughed. "I went out with some goofy boys in high school, but I don't think I knew anyone quite that knuckleheaded."

Abby pretended to laugh, too. "Yeah, I guess that would be pretty dumb," she said, and quickly got busy with her bagel again.

"This doesn't have anything to do with the dance on Friday, does it?" her dad asked. "Did someone ask you? I thought you and Chelsea were going together."

"No — I mean, yes," Abby mumbled with her mouth full. She chewed slowly, using the time to think. She didn't want her parents to know what a knucklehead *she'd* been. "That is, yes, Chelsea and I are planning to go together. And no, nobody's asked me," she said finally. It wasn't *un*true.

"Is that what's bothering you? Oh, hon, I wouldn't worry too much about not having a date," her mom said, stirring milk into her coffee. "For Pete's sake, you're only eleven! Just go and have a good time with your friends."

I wish I could! Abby thought mournfully.

"You have more important stuff to think about, anyway," her dad chimed in. "Speaking of which, how's your speech for the school election coming along?"

"I was planning on working on it today," Abby told him, glad to get off the subject of the dance. The speech had been hanging over Abby's head ever since she'd signed up to run for treasurer. The assembly was on Wednesday, and she still hadn't figured out what she was going to say.

"Well, I'd be glad to hear it when you're done," her dad said. "It's a good idea to practice a few times in front of an audience, just so you get the hang of it."

"Thanks, Dad," Abby said, getting up from the table. "I will."

In her room, she sat down at her desk and took out a blank piece of notebook paper. She stared at it until the blue lines started to blur. But she couldn't concentrate. Her mind kept sliding back to the Matt-Marcus problem.

A beep on her phone startled her. Abby picked it up and saw she had a new message.

LIBRA: YOU MAY FEEL PULLED IN DIFFERENT DIRECTIONS TODAY. TAKE A BREAK AND CLEAR YOUR MIND. INSPIRATION WILL STRIKE!

She's right! Abby thought. *What I need to do is forget about all this dance stuff for a while.*

Abby went over to her bed and lay down. She closed her eyes and waited for inspiration to strike.

She stayed like that for a long time, but nothing happened.

Maybe what I need is some relaxing music, she thought, sitting up. She found her MP3 player and selected some chill R&B. As a woman's smooth voice crooned through her headphones, Abby leaned back on her pillows.

"... Oh, one man is cool and discreet," the woman sang, "but the other is oh, so sweet. How do I choose, so I don't lose . . ."

Oops! Abby thought. *Not what I want to hear right now.* She skipped ahead to another track.

"You're the one I'll take a chance with. The only one I'll ever dance with. . . ."

Abby yanked off the headphones. "Okay, maybe music is not what I need right now," she said to herself. "How about some TV?"

She went into the den and switched on the television. But it was Sunday afternoon, and there wasn't much on. She flipped through golf tournaments, cooking shows, old western movies, commercials. . . .

Abby's dad wandered into the room. "I thought you were working on your speech," he said when he saw her.

"I'm trying to get inspired," she told him.

He eyed the infomercial she was watching. "Unless you're planning on selling the sixth graders a Japanese knife set, I doubt you'll get many ideas there," he said.

"I'm *relaxing* so I can get inspired," Abby explained.

"I see." Mr. Waterman picked up the newspaper and began to sort through it, looking for the sports section. "Who was it that said invention is ten percent inspiration and ninety percent perspiration?"

"Eww." Abby wrinkled her nose. "Obviously a very sweaty person."

Abby's phone rang. She looked at the caller ID but didn't recognize the number. "Hello?" she answered cautiously.

"Ehhhh, hello!" came an annoying, nasal voice. "Ehhhh, may I speak to a Miss Abby Waterman?"

"Who is this, please?" said Abby.

"Ehhhhh, this is Ima Gasser from the Clorox Clearing House Sweepstakes," the person on the other end whined. "I'm calling to tell you you've won two hundred cases of toilet bowl cleaner."

"I'm sorry," Abby said. "I didn't enter any sweepstakes." Her dad glanced up from the newspaper and raised his eyebrows. Abby shrugged to say she didn't know what was going on.

"So, ehhhhhh, can we bring over the dump truck with your toilet bowl cleaner?" His voice was so awful it made Abby cringe.

"I don't know what you're talking about," she said. "I have to go now."

The person on the other end of the line started to laugh. "Abby," he said, "it's Marcus!"

"Oh. Marcus." Abby sighed. "I didn't recognize your number." She picked up the remote and began to flip through the TV channels again.

"I'm calling from the land line," Marcus explained in his normal voice. "So, what's going on?"

"Not much. Listen, I can't really talk," Abby said. "I'm, um . . . busy working on my election speech right now."

Behind his newspaper, Abby's dad cleared his throat. Abby scowled at him.

"Election speech?" said Marcus. "Why? Are you running for president or something?"

"Treasurer," Abby told him. "Seventh grade class treasurer."

"What for?"

"What?" Abby said, startled. What kind of question was that?

"I mean, no offense, but it sounds kind of lame," Marcus said. "What does a treasurer even do?"

"They do lots of things! Like . . . like . . ." Suddenly, Abby realized she wasn't quite sure what a treasurer did. "Stuff with money," she finished lamely.

Marcus laughed. "See? You don't even know!"

"I do too know." Abby's mind was racing. She didn't want to admit that Marcus was right. "They, um . . . they help to organize class fund-raisers, for example." She didn't know if this was true. But why couldn't it be?

"Fund-raisers for what?" asked Marcus.

"You know, so the class can get stuff they want like, um . . ." Abby chewed her lip, trying to think of something cool. A soccer game on the TV suddenly gave her an idea. "A foosball table in the cafeteria," she told Marcus.

"Seriously? That would be awesome!" Marcus said.

Abby smiled. It *was* a pretty good idea. They'd had a foosball table in the lunchroom at her old school, and it had been super-popular.

"Would they really let us have a foosball table in the cafeteria?" Marcus asked.

"I'm not sure," Abby admitted. "But if we raised the money to buy it, how could they say no?"

"Money talks," agreed Marcus.

"Yeah," Abby laughed. "And there are other things kids are always saying they want more of . . . like dances and stuff."

Ooh! Abby slapped her forehead. Why did she have to go and bring up the dance? It was the last thing she wanted to talk to Marcus about right now.

"Anyway," Abby said, her tone becoming businesslike. "As you can see, I have a lot to think about. So I'd really better get back to work."

"Good luck with that," Marcus said. "I guess I'll see you at school tomorrow."

Abby had just hung up with Marcus, when her phone rang again. It was Chelsea.

"Are you doing anything right now?" Chelsea asked.

Abby went back to flipping through the channels on the TV. "Just surfing and waiting for lightning to strike," she said.

"What?"

"I'm watching TV and trying to get inspiration for my speech," Abby told her.

"Well, I have something that will totally inspire you," Chelsea said. She sounded excited. "Can I come over?"

"Sure," Abby said, feeling hopeful. Maybe Chelsea would have some ideas for pulling her speech together!

Twenty minutes later, Chelsea was on Abby's doorstep. She had her backpack slung over her shoulders. "What's in there? Your homework?" Abby asked.

"As if!" Chelsea said, rolling her eyes. "Come on, let's go to your room. I'll show you!"

As soon as they were in Abby's room, Chelsea shut the door. "So what's the big secret?" Abby asked.

"It's not really a secret. But look what I got this morning!" Chelsea dumped her backpack out onto Abby's bed. Tubes of mascara, eyeliner pencils, and little cases of eye shadow and blush spilled out onto the bedspread.

Abby stared at the pile of makeup. "What did you do? Rob the samples counter at Macy's?"

Chelsea giggled. "I borrowed it from Tori," she said. Tori was Chelsea's older sister.

Abby examined a little palette of eye shadow. The frosty pink, cream, and brown squares reminded her of tubs of ice cream in an ice-cream store. "So you're going to start wearing makeup?" she asked.

"It's for the dance!" Chelsea told her. "I thought we could practice now, so it'll look perfect for the big night."

"I don't know," Abby said. "I mean, it sounds fun and everything. But I really need to work on my speech today."

"You should probably wear some makeup when you give your speech, too. Just a little lipstick and blush, maybe," Chelsea said, plucking a little round case of blush from the pile. "Did you know that most politicians wear makeup when they go on TV? It's true, even men!"

Abby shuddered, remembering her lipstick mishap with Matt. "No lipstick, thanks. I'm sticking to clear gloss from now on," she told Chelsea.

Chelsea's lower lip stuck out in a pout. "I thought you'd be more excited," she said to Abby.

"It's really cool," Abby said quickly. "It's just . . ." How could she explain to her best friend that makeup didn't seem all that important when there was so much else going on?

"Listen," said Chelsea, "let's practice putting on makeup for the dance, and then I'll help you with your speech."

Abby glanced guiltily at the blank sheet of paper on her desk. *But I am supposed to take a break and get my mind off things,* she reminded herself. *And then inspiration will strike!*

She turned to Chelsea and smiled. "Okay," she said. "Let's get beautiful."

⋆ Chapter Seven ⋆

"Come on, Mom. I'm going to be late for school," Abby said on Monday morning.

Mrs. Waterman was standing in the kitchen with the cordless phone tucked between her shoulder and her ear, listening to her voice mail messages. "Oh, for Pete's sake!" she snapped, hanging up abruptly.

"What's wrong?" Abby asked as she found her coat and backpack.

Her mother sighed and ran a hand through her hair. "It's the party I'm catering this weekend. They ordered pecan tartlets, so I went out and bought forty dollars' worth of pecans. But suddenly they've changed their minds. Now they want cheesecake!"

"Cheesecake?" Abby murmured. Something

91

was ringing a bell. "Oh my gosh!" she gasped. "The bake sale!"

Her mother finished zipping up her jacket. "Bake sale?"

"The track team bake sale is today, and I didn't make anything!" Abby couldn't believe she'd forgotten something so important. "Can we pick something up at the store on the way to school, Mom? Please?"

Mrs. Waterman checked her watch. "We're already running late as it is," she said.

"Then could you buy something for me and drop it off before lunch?" Abby begged.

"I have to be at an appointment all the way across town this morning," her mom said, shaking her head. "I hate to say this, Abby, but you had all weekend to make something."

"I forgot, Mom. It wasn't on purpose. I just got busy working on my speech yesterday," Abby replied, feeling a stab of guilt. The truth was, she and Chelsea had never really gotten around to working on her campaign speech. They had given each other makeovers until almost dinnertime, and after that, Abby had homework to finish.

But the assembly wasn't until Wednesday. Right now the bake sale was more important. She couldn't stand the thought of letting the track team down again. "Isn't there anything I can take?" she asked her mom.

"Well . . ." Mrs. Waterman pursed her lips. "I think there might be some mini apple turnovers down in the freezer. They were left over from a party I catered last month. Mind you, they're better when they're heated up. . . ."

Abby didn't need to hear more. She was sprinting down to the basement before her mother had even finished her sentence.

The Watermans' basement was an unfinished room that they used mostly for storage. At the back there was a large brown freezer where Mrs. Waterman kept extra supplies for her catering business. A first glance through it turned up only jars of jam, frozen vegetables, and several bags of pecans. But after a little digging, Abby found two gallon-sized Ziploc bags full of triangular pastries.

Abby grabbed both bags and dashed back up the stairs. "Found 'em!" she told her mom as she stuffed the bags into her backpack.

"As I was saying, they'd be a lot better if you could heat them up," her mother said as she picked up the car keys.

"I'll let them defrost in my locker," Abby told her, slipping her backpack over her shoulder. "I'm sure they'll be absolutely perfect."

When the bell rang at the end of math class, Abby was the first one out of her seat. She wanted to get to the cafeteria early so she could help set up for the bake sale.

She had just reached the door, when Marcus came up behind her. "Hey, Abby."

Abby braced herself, waiting for him to step on the backs of her shoes or make an embarrassing noise or something.

"How'd your speech go yesterday?" Marcus asked. He actually sounded interested.

"Okay," Abby lied, starting to walk faster. She was beginning to realize that Marcus could be a normal person when he wanted to be — which only made her feel worse about what she had to do. Because Abby had decided she was definitely going to the dance with Matt, which meant that eventually she was going to have to tell Marcus the truth.

But not today, Abby thought, remembering her horoscope. She'd read it right after first period that morning, and as usual it had given her the answer she needed.

LIBRA: TRY NOT TO MAKE ANY WAVES TODAY. YOU'RE ALREADY NAVIGATING ROUGH WATERS AS IT IS. YOUR BEST BET IS TO GO WITH THE FLOW TO KEEP THINGS ON AN EVEN KEEL.

"So, I was wondering," Marcus said, hurrying to keep up with her. "What . . . uh, what color is the dress you're wearing to the dance?"

"I don't have a dress yet," she told Marcus truthfully. At the mall on Saturday, she and Chelsea had spent the rest of the afternoon with Nathan and Matt. They'd never gotten around to finding a dress for Abby. "Why do you want to know?"

Marcus looked uncomfortable. "Well, Trish — you know, my sister — she says I'm supposed to get you a corsage, and uh . . . I guess it has to match your dress."

Abby was so surprised that she stopped in her tracks. Marcus almost bumped into her. "No, Marcus." She shook her head. "You definitely should not get me a corsage."

Tell him, said a little voice in her head. *Here's your chance. Tell him now!*

Not today, another voice reasoned. *Don't make waves. Just go with the flow.*

"Yeah." Marcus gave a little embarrassed laugh. "I told Trish she was just being stupid. But she said I should ask you, anyway. I'll catch you later, all right?" And before Abby could say anything else, he shuffled off down the hall.

Abby groaned and leaned back against her locker. *This is starting to get out of hand!* she thought.

Just then, Chelsea came hurrying up to her. "Abby! There you are. I was afraid you'd gone to lunch already."

Chelsea fished a tube of lip gloss out of her bag and used Abby's locker mirror to apply it. Abby had to duck around her to put her books inside. "So, I was thinking," Chelsea said, "we should sit with Nathan and Matt at lunch today. Since we're all sort of couples now."

"Couples?!" Abby straightened up so quickly she hit her head on her locker shelf again. "*Ow!* Who said we were couples?" she asked Chelsea, rubbing her head.

"We *are* going to the dance together," Chelsea pointed out.

"But that doesn't make you a couple, does it?" Abby wasn't sure she was ready to be a couple with Matt. And if asking someone to a dance made you a couple, did that mean she and Marcus were a couple, too?

"I guess not officially," Chelsea admitted. "But it definitely makes you *something*. You know, Tori told me she had her first kiss at a McKinley Spring Dance," she added with an impish smile.

Now there was kissing to worry about, too? Abby put her hands to her temples. Her head had started to throb, and not just because she'd smacked it.

"I can't have lunch with the guys today, Chelsea," she said. "I'm helping out with the track team bake sale."

"Can't you get out of it?" Chelsea asked.

Abby shook her head. "I promised."

Chelsea gave an irritated little huff. "Well, I suppose we could eat lunch with the guys tomorrow," she said reluctantly. She looked back at the mirror, then stopped and sniffed. "Did you bring a tuna fish sandwich to school today?"

"No way," Abby said. "You know I hate tuna."

"Well, your locker smells kind of funky."

Abby stuck her nose into the locker and sniffed. Chelsea was right. It did smell a little fishy. "That's weird. Maybe it's Tony's lunch," she said, pointing to the locker next door.

"Ew, you're probably right," said Chelsea. "He's such a slob. I wouldn't be surprised if he had a three-week-old tuna sandwich buried somewhere in there."

"I'd better get going." Abby grabbed the bags of turnovers out of her backpack. "You'll stop by the bake sale and keep me company, right?"

"Sure." Chelsea had turned back to the mirror and was busy fixing her bangs.

"Cool," said Abby. "See you then."

In the cafeteria, two long folding tables had been set up at the back of the room. A handmade banner across the front read SUPPORT THE M.M.S. TRACK TEAM! in orange and blue letters. Suz, Olu, and a long-distance runner named Jamie were standing behind the tables, setting out plates of treats.

Abby hesitated by the door of the lunchroom, nervously clutching the Ziploc bags. This was the first time she'd seen any of the girls since the meet. She wondered if her track splat was as fresh in their minds as it was in hers.

You can't stand here all day, she reminded herself. She walked over and set the bags of turnovers down on the table. "Hi, guys," she said cautiously.

Jamie looked up from a plate of brownies she was unwrapping. "Hey, Abby."

"Oh, good," Olu said. "I'm glad you're here, Rabbit. Can you start putting out some of those cookies?" She nodded toward a bunch of tins stacked beneath the table.

Abby breathed a sigh of relief. Everyone was acting normal. Maybe they weren't going to hold it against her after all.

"Look at all this stuff!" Abby said as she began to unpack cookies. It was hard to find a place to put everything. The tables were already crowded with brownies, muffins, Rice Krispies Treats, and cakes.

"I know!" Jamie beamed. "The team totally came through."

"What did you bring, Rabbit?" asked Suz, who was writing out prices on a sheet of paper.

"Mini apple turnovers." Abby began to unload the treats onto a paper plate. "My mom made them. She's a professional caterer," she added proudly.

"Cool," said Suz. "How much do you think we should charge for them?"

"They're kind of small," Abby said. "How about twenty-five cents for two?"

Suz nodded and added them to the price list. A few kids had started to wander over. They picked out brownies, cookies, and lemon squares, handing over quarters and dollars. Olu collected the money and put it in a metal box.

"How's the bake sale going?" Krista asked, walking up. She selected a brownie from one of the plates, then leaned against the edge of the table, nibbling at her treat and talking to the other girls. She didn't even glance in Abby's direction.

Abby wasn't surprised. She didn't expect Krista to suddenly start being friendly to her. But it still bugged her how Krista always acted like she was in charge. *I hope she plans to pay for that brownie!* Abby thought.

"Which are the apple turnovers?" asked a boy standing in front of Abby. He was reading over the price list. Abby pointed to the pastries.

"I'll take four." The boy handed over two quarters. Abby gave him the turnovers in a paper napkin.

The boy popped one in his mouth. A second later it came flying back out.

"Ugh!" he cried. "There's something wrong with these things."

Abby's eyes widened. "What are you talking about? There's nothing wrong with them!"

"Have you tried one?" the boy countered.

Abby picked up a turnover and took a tentative nibble. The minute she bit down, she knew the boy was right. There was something seriously wrong with the turnovers. The filling was fleshy and pink and a little fishy tasting. It wasn't apple . . . it was shrimp!

Oh no! Abby groaned inwardly. *I must have grabbed the wrong bags from the freezer!*

The boy wiped his tongue with the paper napkin. "I want my money back," he said loudly.

"What's going on?" asked Olu, coming to Abby's side.

"She poisoned me!" the boy exclaimed. "She said those things were apple turnovers, but they've got some weird slimy stuff in them."

"Shrimp, actually," Abby said meekly.

"Gross!" The boy held out his hand. "That's false advertising. You owe me fifty cents."

Everyone was watching them now. Krista laughed, her eyes glittering. "You brought *shrimp* turnovers to a bake sale, Abby?"

Abby was too mortified to reply. She silently placed two quarters in the boy's palm. "Better give me another quarter," he said. "I have to go buy a Coke to wash the taste out of my mouth."

Abby glanced over at the other girls. "Just give it to him," Olu said, rolling her eyes.

Abby pulled a quarter out of her own pocket and handed it to the boy. He walked away smiling and jingling the change.

"Nice going, Abby," Krista sneered. "Now we're actually *losing* money."

We? I don't see you helping out! Abby thought angrily. It was one thing to be mad about the race. But Krista was just being nasty now. Abby was dying to say something, but she bit back the words. *"Don't make waves today,"* she reminded herself. *"Just go with the flow."*

More kids trickled over to the table to buy cookies and brownies. Krista pointed out the shrimp turnovers every chance she got, and Abby felt more and more embarrassed. She wished Chelsea would come over so she'd have someone to talk to. But she seemed to have forgotten her promise to stop by.

By halfway through the lunch period, the bake-sale tables were still loaded with treats. "This stuff isn't selling fast enough," Jamie complained. "What are we going to do with it all?"

"Take it home, I guess," said Suz.

"My mom's on a diet. She'll kill me if I bring home ten pounds of cookies," said Olu.

"Well, maybe we can give it to a homeless shelter or something," said Suz.

"But then we won't make any money for the track," Jamie pointed out. "It will all have been for nothing."

Abby chewed her thumbnail, staring gloomily into space. She didn't care what they did with the treats. She just wanted it to be over.

Abby had just decided to tip the shrimp turn-overs into the trash, when she heard a familiar voice say, "What's up, dude?"

Abby looked up. Matt was standing next to the table, peering down at her through his floppy bangs.

"Hey!" Abby exclaimed, jumping to her feet. This was the first time Matt had ever come up to her at school. "We're having a bake sale for the track team. Do you want to buy a cookie? Or maybe a Rice Krispies Treat?"

Matt looked the goodies over. "Which ones did you bring?" he asked Abby.

He would have to ask that, Abby thought. She considered pointing to a nice-looking lemon cake, but Olu and Suz were listening with rapt attention. Abby was afraid they'd call her out if she fibbed.

"I brought those . . . shrimp turnovers," she mumbled.

Matt blinked. "Did you say *shrimp*?"

Abby nodded miserably.

"Dude," said Matt. "That's weird." He bought a chocolate-chip cookie and moved on.

As soon as he was gone, Suz and Olu pounced. "Sooo, Rabbit," Suz said, grinning. "What's up between you and Matt Anderson?"

"Nothing," Abby said. "We're just, um, maybe going to the dance together."

"'Maybe'?" Olu raised one eyebrow. "You don't sound very excited about it."

"Oh, I am," Abby assured her. "But . . . it's complicated."

Right then, Abby spotted the main complication coming toward her, a big smile stretched across his freckled face. *Oh no,* Abby thought. *Not Marcus again.*

"I heard there's a seafood special over here," Marcus joked as he walked up.

"Very funny," Abby said glumly.

"You really do have some cutting-edge ideas, Abby," Marcus said. He slid a quarter across the table. "I'll take two."

"You don't have to do that," Abby told him. "I was just about to throw them away."

"I like shrimp." He plucked one off the pile, tossed it high into the air, and caught it in his mouth.

"Very impressive," Abby said. "What is it with you and food tricks?"

Marcus shrugged. "That's nothing. Watch this." He took several steps back, until he was about ten feet away. "Okay, now you throw one to me. Go ahead."

Feeling silly, Abby took a shrimp turnover and gave it an underhand toss. It arced through the air . . . and landed in Marcus's mouth.

"Wow!" Abby said. "How'd you learn to do that?"

Marcus smiled mysteriously. "I'm a man of many talents," he said.

Sure, Abby thought. *And most of them are weird!*

"Hey, that was cool. Do it again," said Jamie, who'd been watching.

Marcus glanced at Abby and raised one eyebrow. "You'll have to buy the shrimp turnover first," he told Jamie.

"Okay." Jamie tossed a quarter into the metal box, then grabbed two shrimp turnovers. She pitched them at Marcus, faster than Abby had. He managed to catch both.

Jamie laughed. "Right on! You're like a trained seal. And I mean that as a compliment," she added.

"Arf! Arf!" said Marcus, slapping his hands together like flippers.

They had started to draw a crowd. Soon more kids were laying down quarters to buy shrimp turnovers. It seemed that no one could resist the opportunity to throw food at Marcus.

"This is great. We're raking it in!" Olu said gleefully. Kids were buying the other treats, too, and the plates on the tables were emptying rapidly.

Marcus is a total weirdo, Abby thought, watching as he caught half a cookie in his mouth. *But he's also kind of brilliant in his own strange way.*

Just then, Chelsea walked up. "What's going on?" she asked Abby.

"Check out Marcus. He's saving the bake sale," Abby said.

They watched as Marcus did a 360-degree spin before catching another turnover in his mouth.

"Gosh, he is *so* desperate for attention," Chelsea remarked.

"I don't think he's so bad," Abby said.

"Please, Abby. He should be in a zoo," Chelsea replied.

"Out of the way! Out of the way!" a voice boomed. Kids scattered left and right as Ms. Jenkins came bulldozing her way through the crowd. She stopped in front of the table and planted her hands on her hips. "What's going on here?"

Abby and the other girls froze. Marcus, who'd just caught another turnover in his mouth, swallowed with a loud gulp.

"It's . . . it's just a bake sale," Abby suddenly spoke up, surprised at her own nerve. "Would you like a piece of cake, Ms. Jenkins? It's on the house." Abby held out a piece of frosted lemon cake wrapped in a paper napkin.

The monitor's eyes shifted from Abby to the cake. "Well," she sniffed after a moment, "that would be very nice."

"Have a brownie, too," said Suz, piling one on top of the cake.

"And a toffee-chip cookie," said Olu, adding it to the stack.

"Okay, that's enough, girls. That's enough." Ms. Jenkins giggled. "Have to watch the waistline, you know," she added, patting her thick middle.

As the monitor walked away with her treats, Suz high-fived Abby. "Nice one, Rabbit!"

"That was awesome," Jamie agreed.

"Yeah, Abby should win a big award," Krista said nastily. "First place for kissing up."

The grin faded from Abby's face. It seemed like

no matter what she did, Krista would find some-thing to pick on. Abby knew she shouldn't care. But it still stung.

"Forget her," Olu told Abby as Krista walked away. "She'll be psyched when we get that new track. Look how much money we made!" She pointed to the metal box, which was overflowing with coins and bills.

"Maybe we should give Marcus a cut," Abby said. "For his promotional help."

Marcus shook his head. "That's okay. I got a free lunch out of it. Although," he added, putting a hand on his stomach, "I don't think I'll be eating any more shrimp for a long, long time."

⋆ Chapter Eight ⋆

"Abby, hold your hand steady!" Coach Nelson shouted. "Your arm's flapping all over the place."

Abby tried to make her arm rigid as she started to run. She could hear Suz coming up behind her. Abby groped for the baton and felt it brush her fingers. But she couldn't get a grip. As soon as Suz let go, the baton fell to the ground.

Both runners slowed to a stop. Abby turned and saw Krista, Suz, and Olu all looking at her. Krista's arms were crossed, and Olu had her hands on her hips. As soon as Krista met Abby's eye, she looked down at the ground and spit.

"Abby," said Coach Nelson, "don't feel for the baton. Just keep your hand steady and it will be there. Okay, let's try it again, guys."

"Coach, that's the fourth time Abby's dropped it today," Krista spoke up.

The coach frowned. "Well, then it's a good thing this is just practice, isn't it? Take your places, and let's try it again," he repeated.

Krista narrowed her eyes and whispered something to Olu, who nodded. Abby swallowed hard. They'd been drilling handoffs for most of practice, and so far she hadn't gotten it right once. But the harder she tried to make things go right, the more she seemed to screw up.

The relay team tried the handoff once more. And once again, Abby fumbled it.

"Okay," said Coach Nelson. "Let's take a break. You guys get some water. Abby, can I talk to you for a minute?"

As the other girls went to grab their water bottles, Abby slowly walked over to the coach. She had a feeling this talk wasn't going to go well.

"What's going on?" the coach asked. "You had this stuff down last week, and today it's like you've never seen a baton in your life."

"It's just..." Abby hesitated. Should she explain about her horoscope? *Coach,* she imagined herself saying, *it's just cosmically impossible for me to connect today. You know how it goes.*

Probably better to keep it simple, she decided. "I guess I'm just having an off day," she told him.

That was the understatement of the century. It seemed like nothing had gone right for her all day. First thing that morning, Chelsea had been obsessing about the dance again. She'd been on Abby's case about not having a dress yet. Then she'd started in on something called boutonnieres, which sounded to Abby like an old-time disease, but turned out to be flowers they were supposed to pin to the boys' jackets. "We have to order them today!" Chelsea had said, like it was a real emergency. Abby had hinted that maybe Chelsea was going a little overboard, and they'd almost gotten into a fight.

Then at lunch, she and Chelsea had sat at the seventh grade table with Nathan and Matt. Abby had made a dumb joke about football, and everyone had looked at her like she was from outer space. And *then* Marcus had walked over, and Abby had to run and hide in the girls' bathroom so he wouldn't say anything about the dance in front of Chelsea and Matt. After that, Abby didn't see Marcus again, so she hadn't had the chance to explain that the dance was off.

All in all, it had been a horrible day. Abby couldn't wait until it was over.

The coach studied Abby from beneath the brim of his baseball cap. "Everyone has off days, Abby. But I get the feeling that you're not really trying."

"I *am* trying. I think I just need to try again at a better time," she quoted from her horoscope.

The coach's eyebrows shot up. "A better time? What's a better time? Do you think it will be a *better time* at the meet on Friday?"

Abby was silent. How could she know what Friday would be like?

"Look, you're a good runner, but you have to get your head in the game," the coach told her. "It's not just you in a relay. There are three other people counting on you. If you can't show that you're doing your best, then for their sake I'm going to have to pull you from the relay team."

Abby toed the grass with her sneaker. "I'm sure they'd all like that," she mumbled.

Coach Nelson folded his arms. "Is this all about what happened last Friday?" he asked.

"I really blew it at the meet," Abby said.

"Well, get over it. Running is seventy percent mental." He tapped a finger to his forehead. "It's all up here. You can be a great runner, but if you psych yourself out, you're never going to win."

Abby thought about that. What her coach was saying made sense. But what if she set out to win on a day she was destined to lose? If the stars were already crossed against her, what could she possibly do? And if she was destined to win, wouldn't she win whether she'd practiced hard or not?

But not trying didn't seem right to Abby either. What was the point of doing anything if you weren't at least going to try? Abby went back and forth, but she didn't know which way was right.

"So, you ready to get back out there and give it another go?" Coach Nelson asked.

Abby took a deep breath. "I'll give it my best shot," she said. It seemed like that was all she could do.

When track practice was over that day, Abby found a message on her phone from her mom. Mrs. Waterman had been held up at an appointment and was running late. She wouldn't be there for a half hour at least.

"A half hour?" Abby groaned. With everything else that had been going on, she hadn't managed to eat much of her lunch that day. Now she was ravenous.

She called her mother back and told her she was going over to 8th Street to get a snack, and that she should pick her up there instead of at school.

Eighth Street was a two-block strip of little shops and cafés just around the corner from McKinley. Abby bought a frozen yogurt sundae, then sat on the bench outside to eat it.

As she spooned up a bite, Abby noticed a new shop across the street. Thick purple curtains hung in the windows. A small blue neon sign proclaimed: ASTROLOGY READINGS. NO APPOINTMENT NECESSARY.

Abby froze, the spoon still in her mouth. If that sign meant what she thought it meant, then there was a real, live astrologer across the street. Maybe *she* could tell Abby what to do about the mess she was in.

Abby quickly finished the rest of her yogurt, dumped the cup in the trash, and hurried across the street.

Bells on the door jingled when Abby pushed it open. As she stepped inside the tiny room, Abby looked around in surprise. She didn't know what she expected an astrologer's place to be like, but it certainly wasn't this. Aside from the purple curtains, it looked like any old office — gray carpet, potted plants, a few paintings on the walls. Behind a large messy desk, a woman sat working on a computer.

The woman looked up when Abby walked in. She had curly red hair piled in a loose bun. Her glasses were hanging from her neck on a beaded chain.

"Hello, dear," the woman said, smiling. Her eyes, magnified by her thick glasses, looked watery and enormous. "You're early, but that's just fine."

Abby stared at her in amazement. "You knew I was coming?"

"Of course." The woman consulted a calendar on her desk. "I have you down here for five-fifteen. Ariel Freeman, right?"

"Oh," said Abby, suddenly understanding. "No, I don't have an appointment."

"A walk-in? Lovely. But unfortunately I only have twenty minutes before my next client. Maybe you'd like to come back?" She looked at her calendar again. "We could schedule an appointment for next week."

Abby shook her head. "That won't do any good. See, I really need help now."

"Ah, I see." The woman nodded knowingly. "Mercury troubles."

"Huh?" said Abby.

The woman sighed. "Ever since Mercury went into retrograde, I've been absolutely swamped. Everyone wants to know when it's going direct so they can get on with their lives."

It was as if the woman was speaking another language. "I, um, just wanted to know about my horoscope," Abby said uncertainly.

The woman clapped her hands together. "Oh, a first-timer! My mistake. Well, sit down, dear. Sit down. We can work up a quick chart for you."

Abby glanced around, but she didn't see a price list anywhere. "Does that cost a lot? Because I don't have much money. . . ."

"Normally, I charge fifty dollars a session," the woman said. "But we don't have much time. I can do a quick chart interpretation for twenty."

Twenty dollars? Abby thought. That was exactly the amount she'd found in the school parking lot last week. Abby still had the bill tucked in her wallet. She'd been saving it for the right occasion — and it seemed like the time was now.

Abby sat in a wooden chair across from the woman's desk. The woman turned to her computer. "Your name?" she asked.

"Abby Waterman," said Abby.

The woman smiled at her over the top of her glasses. "I'm Connie Bloch," she said. Once again, Abby was surprised. "Connie Bloch" sounded a lot less exotic than "Miz Astrid."

Connie Bloch asked Abby more questions, like her birth date and where she was born and what time of the day. She typed all the answers into the computer. A moment later, the printer spit out a chart.

"Ah, the wonders of modern technology," the astrologer sighed. "When I first started in this field, you had to do everything by hand. It took ages!" She pushed the paper across the desk to Abby. "There, my dear. That's your natal chart. It shows the position of all the planets on the day you were born."

Abby studied the chart. It looked sort of like a dial, with a lot of numbers and squiggles inside.

"Now let's see." Connie Bloch took the chart back, settling her glasses higher on her nose. "Your sun sign is five degrees Libra. But you probably already know that you're a Libra. Everyone knows their sun sign, but they don't always know what it means. Libras are lovely — charming and attractive. They always see both sides of a situation, which can make them indecisive. I suppose you have a bit of trouble making decisions. Am I right?" She raised an eyebrow questioningly, and Abby nodded.

Connie Bloch tapped a long purple fingernail at a dot on the chart. "Your rising sign is seventeen degrees Virgo — that means you're a thinker! Organized, too. I'll bet you always do all your homework. Moon is eight degrees Capricorn. And let's see . . . Mercury five degrees Leo; Mars in Aries . . ."

Once again, Connie Bloch seemed to be speaking gibberish. Abby glanced at her watch. There were only a few minutes left before the astrologer's next appointment arrived, and they still hadn't gotten around to the real reason she was there.

"What's the matter, dear?" Connie Bloch had stopped reading. She was looking at Abby over the top of the paper.

"Well . . ." Abby bit her lip. "It's just that I don't understand anything that you're saying," she admitted. "And I have this big problem." Then Abby launched into the whole story, how she'd promised Chelsea she'd ask Matt, but she'd accidentally asked Marcus, and then she'd ended up asking Matt, anyway. Connie Bloch listened carefully, her eyes widening enormously behind her glasses.

"Goodness!" the astrologer exclaimed when Abby had finished. "You have to fix that, or someone's going to get their feelings hurt!"

"I know," Abby told her. "But how do I fix it? Which one am I supposed to take to the dance?"

Connie Bloch pursed her lips thoughtfully. "Well, I suppose we could look at which sign is most compatible with yours. I don't suppose you know their birthdays, do you?"

Abby shook her head.

"Ah," Connie Bloch nodded. "It's just as well. In my experience, that's not always the best way to make a match. There are so many, many things you can't know just by looking at someone's star sign."

Connie Bloch took off her glasses, then folded her arms on the desk and looked at Abby. "I'm afraid I can't tell you which boy to go to the dance with," she said. "But I can tell you something about Libras. They have a very good sense of right and wrong — more than any other sign in the zodiac. If you're honest with yourself, you'll know the right thing to do."

The bells on the door tinkled, and Connie Bloch looked up. "That's my next appointment."

Abby stood and took the twenty dollars out of her wallet. "Thanks for your help," she said, laying it on the desk.

Connie Bloch smiled and shook her head. "That wasn't astrology, dear. That was just free advice." She put the money back in Abby's hand. "Come back and see me sometime when you want a real reading."

⋆ Chapter Nine ⋆

"Gosh, Abby, you look so nice!" Chelsea exclaimed at school on Wednesday morning.

"Thanks," Abby replied with a grin. She was dressed in her best blue shirt, a crisp khaki skirt, and low-wedge sandals. Her freshly washed hair was twisted into two neat French braids, and her lips shone with just a touch of light pink lip gloss.

Chelsea nodded approvingly. "So are you ready for the assembly?"

Abby nodded. "I was up almost all night working on my speech."

It had taken several drafts, but sometime after midnight Abby finally had something she felt good about. By then her parents were asleep, so she had practiced in front of the bathroom mirror, reciting her speech over and over again until she knew it by heart.

"You're going to be awesome," Chelsea said, giving her a quick hug. "Listen, I'm going to catch up with Sara and Toshi so we can all sit together. Gosh, I love assemblies," she added with a happy sigh. "Getting out of class is the best! See you later, okay?"

As Chelsea headed off down the hall, Abby checked her hair in her locker mirror one last time, running through her speech again in her mind. Just as she was about to shut her locker and head to the gym, her phone beeped. Abby picked it up and saw she had a new text from Daily Horoscopes.

She hesitated with her thumb on the ANSWER button. Should she open it now, or wait until after she'd given her speech?

It's better to know, Abby decided. She pressed the button, and the message blipped up on the phone's display.

DAILY HOROSCOPES BY MIZ ASTRID

LIBRA: DESPITE YOUR BEST INTENTIONS, YOUR PLANS COULD FALL APART TODAY. IF YOU AREN'T CAREFUL, YOU COULD LOSE SOMETHING IMPORTANT TO YOU.

Abby went cold all over. She read the message again, but there was no mistaking its meaning: She was going to mess up her speech and lose the election.

Abby put the phone back in her locker. All the nervous excitement she'd felt drained away. It was replaced by a sick, shaky feeling. In just a few minutes, she was going to have to get up in front of the entire school — all her teachers and friends and the kids in her classes — and give a speech that she knew was going to be a disaster.

"Hey, Abby," said a voice next to her.

Abby blinked and realized Marcus was standing beside her locker. She hadn't even heard him walk up. "I just wanted to say good luck today," he told her.

An unhappy laugh escaped Abby's throat. "Thanks, Marcus," she said. "But I don't think luck is going to be much help."

Marcus peered at her. "Are you okay?"

Abby shook her head. "The stars are against me," she explained. "I don't have a chance."

Marcus looked baffled. "What are you talking about?"

Abby checked her watch. "I'd better get going," she told Marcus. "I have an election to lose."

Taking a deep breath, she walked off down the hall to meet her fate.

The bleachers in the school gymnasium were packed. It was the first really warm day of spring, and even with the windows open the room felt stifling. The lazy fans on the ceiling didn't do much to stir the air. As they listened to the candidates' speeches, the sixth and seventh graders fanned themselves with papers, notebooks, or anything else that was handy.

Out on the half-court line, Abby's opponent, Tyson Storey, was standing at a wobbly wooden podium, telling the sixth grade class why they should vote for him. Tyson's speech seemed to involve mostly sports-related jokes. It was getting a lot of laughs, especially from the guys.

Abby stood to the side, trying to focus on her own speech. But her mind kept flashing back to her horoscope. When she closed her eyes, she could almost see it, as if it was emblazoned onto the backs of her eyelids.

There was a burst of applause, and Abby's eyes snapped open. Tyson Storey was making his way back from the podium. There were a few whistles and shouts of "Go, Tyson!"

This was it. She was up next. Abby's whole mouth went dry.

"And our final candidate for seventh grade class treasurer — Abby Waterman," the vice principal announced into the microphone.

Abby's first impulse was to turn and run. But somehow her legs carried her to the podium in the middle of the gym.

As soon as she looked into the bleachers, Abby realized why people practiced speeches in front of an audience, rather than a mirror. Abby's reflection hadn't cared if she made mistakes. But now there were hundreds of pairs of eyes on her. Everyone was waiting to hear what she had to say, and Abby had a feeling they wouldn't be quite as forgiving as her bathroom mirror.

Wow, there are so many people. A few kids snickered, and suddenly Abby realized she'd spoken the words aloud. Blushing, she cleared her throat and tried to get on with her speech.

"I'm Abby Waterman, and I'm . . . uh, running for class treasurer. I'm betting that, uh, a lot of you have some questions about the treasurer, like . . . like . . . um . . ."

Abby's mind went blank. She couldn't remember the next line of her speech. *It's happening!* she thought. *Just like my horoscope said it would. It's all falling apart!*

Abby froze, clutching the sides of the podium. *Think of something!* Abby told herself. *Anything!* But no words would come.

As the silence stretched on, the audience began to shift uncomfortably. A couple of kids giggled. Abby caught a glimpse of Ms. Hill standing at the side of the room. Her dark eyebrows were drawn together in a worried frown.

"Boooo!" someone said, and laughter rippled through the audience. All the teachers scowled in the direction of the heckler, but no one could tell who it was. Abby felt like she was dying a slow death. She wondered if she should just step down from the podium now.

Just then, someone else called out, "Ehhhhhhhh, I have some questions about the class treasurer." It was a familiar, nasal, very annoying voice.

Marcus! Abby thought. *What is he doing?* She managed to pull herself together enough to peep, "What's your question?"

"Well, ehhhhhhhh, my question is: What's the point? Does a treasurer even do anything?" Marcus whined in his Ima Gasser voice. Kids in the audience were laughing in surprise.

Why is he doing this to me? Abby wailed inwardly. *He knows that's not true! I already explained to him what —*

Suddenly, Abby understood. Marcus wasn't making fun of her. He was trying to get her to remember what she'd told him on the phone. He wanted to help her out!

"Well, uh, I'm glad you asked that," Abby said. Even to her own ears, her voice sounded uncertain, but she plowed ahead. "Maybe treasurers haven't done much in the past. But I think, um . . . I think that should change. If I'm elected treasurer, I promise to work to build up the class treasury."

"*What* class treasury?" someone hollered out, no doubt inspired by Marcus's example.

"The money that belongs to the seventh grade class," Abby said. "I don't think there's much now. But we could make it bigger, and then we could use it to get the things we want, like . . ." She sought out Marcus's eyes, and he gave her a nod. "Maybe a foosball table for the cafeteria," Abby finished.

The audience erupted into murmurs. Apparently, lots of kids liked the idea of a foosball table. Abby glanced over at the principal and vice principal, who were both frowning.

"Or other things, too," Abby added quickly. "The point is, if we *have* a class treasury, then we might have a better chance of getting some of the things we want, because we can use our own money to get them."

Abby took a deep breath. She was feeling more confident now. "Just this week I helped organize a bake sale for the track team," she told the audience. "We earned three hundred and twenty-one dollars, and all of that money will help go toward getting the school a better track. If I'm elected, I promise to hold more fund-raisers for the seventh grade class treasury, and to do my best to get the things you want."

"More dances!" someone shouted.

"Air-conditioning in the gym!" added another voice. Everyone laughed.

"No school on Fridays!" whined Ima/Marcus. Kids laughed even harder.

"Well, I can't promise all that," Abby said, smiling. "But I'll do my best." Ms. Hill was tapping her watch, indicating that Abby had run out of time. Abby quickly wrapped it up. "So vote for me, Abby!"

The audience burst into applause. Abby realized she was clutching the sides of the podium so tightly that her knuckles were white. She pried her fingers off and walked back to the side of the room, her knees shaking.

There were a few whistles and shouts. Abby couldn't tell if the applause was louder than it had been for Tyson, but for the moment it didn't matter. All that mattered was that she'd gotten through it.

And maybe — just maybe — it hadn't been a total disaster after all.

After the assembly, kids shuffled out of the gymnasium like cattle being herded out of a corral. Abby spotted Marcus among the crowd. "Marcus!" she shouted, waving him over.

He walked up, grinning. "Put her there, Treas," he said, raising his hand. The two slapped a high five.

"But don't call me Treas," Abby told him. "I haven't won the election."

"Whatever," said Marcus. "You owned that place. Tomorrow when they announce the results, you'll be all *woo-hoo*!" He busted into a ridiculous dance move, throwing his hips forward and pumping his arms in the air.

"Marcus, cut it out," Abby said, laughing. Kids were starting to stare. But Marcus kept right on dancing, pulling out some embarrassingly bad hip-hop moves.

"Abby!" Chelsea cried, coming up behind her and giving her a bear hug. "You rocked, girl!" She peered over Abby's shoulder at Marcus. "What's with you, Marcus?" she asked. "Did you finally get accepted into clown school?"

"Nah," Marcus said, flapping his elbows, "just practicing my righteous moves for the dance on Friday."

"Oh yeah?" Chelsea smirked. "Who are you going to the dance with?"

Marcus slowed to a stop in front of them, a confused smile on his face. "With Abby," he said. "Didn't you know?"

Oh no! Abby thought.

Chelsea gave a little laugh. "No you're not. Abby's going to the dance with Matt Anderson."

The smile was fading from Marcus's face. "What?"

"I . . . um . . . I . . ." Abby stuttered.

Chelsea looked at Abby and raised her eyebrows. "You mean you didn't tell him?" When Abby didn't say anything, Chelsea turned back to Marcus. "Abby didn't mean to ask you to the dance," she said flatly. "That text message you got? That was supposed to go to Matt. Abby just hit your name by mistake. By the way, Marcus," Chelsea added, "it's not cool to mess with people's phones."

Marcus looked from Chelsea to Abby. His face was frozen in a strange expression, halfway between embarrassed and angry.

"I was going to tell you —" Abby began.

"Whatever," Marcus said, holding up a hand to show he didn't want to hear it. He started to leave, then stopped and looked back. "By the way," he added, "it's not cool to mess with people's heads either." He turned and walked away for good this time.

"Geez," Chelsea said. "He didn't have to get all bent out of shape."

"Chelsea!" Abby exclaimed. "Why did you do that?"

"Me?" Chelsea looked startled. *"You're* the one who didn't take care of the situation. What did you plan to do, Abby? Call him up on the night of the dance and be like, 'Oh, I forgot to mention, I'm going with someone else'?"

"I didn't know what I was going to do," Abby mumbled in frustration. "I was still trying to figure it out."

Chelsea put her hands on her hips. "Don't tell me you were seriously thinking of going to the dance with Marcus Goober. Abby, he's a total loser!"

Abby felt torn in two. She wanted to defend Marcus. She didn't think he was a loser. But she was afraid if she told Chelsea that, Chelsea would think *she* was a loser.

Chelsea put her arm around Abby's shoulders. "Don't feel bad," she told her. "You should be psyched! Everything is already set with Nathan and Matt, and we're going to have the best night ever. You'll see."

Abby sighed. Chelsea was right, as usual. And at least now she didn't have to worry about Marcus anymore. She was going to the dance with Matt, which was how it was supposed to be all along.

⋆ Chapter Ten ⋆

Thursday morning, Abby sat in her homeroom English class, nervously nibbling her thumbnail. On the crackly overhead speaker, the school vice principal was giving the morning announcements. Any moment now, they would hear the results of the school election.

That morning, Abby had woken with a cloud hanging over her head. She already knew she was going to lose the election — her horoscope yesterday had said as much. Now she dreaded the pitying looks she'd get from her friends, or — worse still — the gloating smirks from people who would be *glad* she'd lost. (Krista sprang to mind.) *Might as well just stamp an "L" for "Loser" on my forehead now,* Abby thought.

On the loudspeaker, there was a pause and the sound of rustling papers. Then the school principal came on. "And now for the results of yesterday's class elections," she said.

Several kids looked right at Abby. She pretended to be busy writing in her notebook, letting her hair fall like a curtain to shield her face. She couldn't stand the idea of everyone staring at her when they made the announcement.

"The ballot counts were very close," the principal was saying, "so every student who ran should feel proud of his or her hard work. . . ."

Please just get on with it, she silently pleaded. Adults always felt like they had to say this kind of stuff, but it didn't make the losers feel any better.

"First up, the seventh grade class representatives," came the principal's voice. "Congratulations to our new seventh grade treasurer . . . Abby Waterman."

Abby's head snapped up. *That's me!* she thought. But . . . that couldn't be right. She was supposed to lose! *They must have counted the ballots wrong,* Abby thought. *Or the principal read the wrong name. Or . . . or . . .* She didn't know what.

The principal was announcing the other new seventh grade reps, but Abby didn't hear a word. She sat, dazed, as kids sitting nearby patted her shoulders and offered their congratulations. As she looked at their smiling faces, it started to sink in. Despite what her horoscope had said, she'd won!

Abby was suddenly bursting with excitement. She couldn't wait to see Chelsea and the rest of her friends. *And Marcus, too,* she thought. She'd been feeling guilty about Marcus since the day before. But this was the perfect reason for them to talk. After all, he'd helped her with her speech. If anyone would be excited that she'd won, it would be Marcus!

As soon as the bell rang, Abby scooped up her books and headed for the door.

"Hey, Abby." A kid named Phillip from her class fell into step beside her. "I just wanted to say that I voted for you yesterday."

"Thanks, Phillip," Abby said with a grin.

Phillip didn't return the smile. "Yeah, but now I wish I hadn't," he said. "I heard how you blew Marcus off just to go to the dance with a seventh grader."

Abby stopped walking. "What? That's not what happened. . . ."

But Phillip wasn't listening. "That was a lousy thing to do," he told Abby. "People like you don't deserve to win." He walked away, shaking his head.

Abby stood rooted to the floor. She felt like she'd just been punched in the stomach. Somewhere, somehow, things had gone seriously wrong!

When Abby got to her locker, Chelsea was waiting for her with a big grin plastered across her face. "Hooray!" she squealed, throwing her arms around her friend. "Congratulations. That's soooo awesome, Abby! "

But Abby didn't feel awesome. Phillip's words kept running through her mind: *People like you don't deserve to win.* Did other kids know what had happened with Marcus? And did they think the same thing?

"What's wrong?" Chelsea asked Abby.

Swallowing around the lump in her throat, Abby told Chelsea what Phillip had said.

"Phillip? You mean Phillip Moore?" Chelsea waved a hand as if Phillip was a fly she was swatting away. "He's a geek! Who cares what he says?"

"But he voted for me," Abby said. "And now he thinks I'm a bad person."

Chelsea took Abby's shoulders and gave her a tiny shake, as if she was trying to wake her up.

"You didn't have a choice," she told her firmly. "No girl in her right mind would choose Marcus Goober over Matt Anderson."

"Gruber," said Abby. "His name's Marcus *Gruber.*"

Chelsea sighed as if Abby was totally hopeless. "I see something that will cheer you up," she said, spinning Abby around. "Look, here comes Matt to congratulate you!"

Sure enough, Matt was walking straight toward them. "Hey, Abby," he said as he came up. "I heard you invited both Marcus Gruber and me to the dance."

"You did?" Abby gulped. Next to her, she felt Chelsea stiffen.

"That's seriously uncool, dude," Matt said. "You, like, disrespected both of us. I don't want to go to the dance with you anymore. Just thought I should let you know." With a toss of his bangs, Matt walked away.

Abby looked after him, stunned. "That was the most words he's ever said to me," she told Chelsea.

"This can't be happening!" Chelsea shrieked. "Go after him. Tell him it's all been a big misunderstanding."

"What good would that do?" Abby asked. She felt stupid, but she was also strangely relieved. "He obviously doesn't want to go with me." *And I don't want to go with him either,* she suddenly realized.

"But the dance is tomorrow!" Chelsea wailed. "How are you going to get a date now?"

Suddenly, Abby had had enough. "Who cares about the stupid dance?" she shouted. "I am so *sick* of hearing about the dance. It's all you ever talk about, Chelsea! You act like it's the most important thing in the world!"

Chelsea's mouth fell open. "I worked so hard. I planned it all perfectly. And now you are ruining everything!" she screamed at Abby. Turning on her heel, Chelsea stormed away.

Kids at the nearby lockers stared. Cheeks burning, Abby turned and pretended to be busy getting her books out of her locker. She saw that the message light on her phone was blinking.

Miz Astrid, Abby thought, picking it up. She hardly felt like she needed to read her horoscope. She could already guess what it would say, something like "Libra: Stay in bed today. You can't do anything right."

Abby opened the message and read:

DAILY HOROSCOPES BY MIZ ASTRID

LIBRA: YOU'RE A SUPERSTAR TODAY — YOU SHINE IN EVERY-THING YOU DO. TODAY IS A GREAT DAY FOR FRIENDSHIPS AND ROMANCE. OTHERS WILL WANT TO BASK IN THE GLOW OF YOUR GOOD ENERGY.

Excuse me? Abby thought. She checked the date and the star sign, but both were correct. It just didn't make sense. How could she have gotten one of her best horoscopes ever — on what was turning out to be one of the worst days of her life?

For the rest of the morning, Abby puzzled over this question. And she kept coming back to the same unsettling thought: What if her horoscope was just plain wrong? And if it was wrong today, did that mean it had been wrong other days, too?

At lunch, Abby didn't bother going to the cafeteria. Instead, she found a quiet corner in the library and took out her cell phone. She began to scroll back through her text messages, finding her horoscopes from the past week.

TAKE A CHANCE ON SOMEONE NEW TODAY, Abby read. THIS COULD BE THE START OF AN EXCITING NEW RELATIONSHIP. That had been her horoscope the day she'd first tried to ask Matt to the dance.

"Well, *that* was sure off base," Abby murmured to herself. Her relationship with Matt hadn't gone anywhere. . . .

Except she hadn't actually asked Matt to the dance that day, Abby suddenly realized. She'd asked Marcus. Had her horoscope been trying to tell her she should take a chance . . . on Marcus?

Abby skipped ahead to Friday, the day of the track meet. BEWARE DISTRACTIONS, her horoscope had read. AN OVERLOOKED DETAIL, NO MATTER HOW SMALL, COULD REALLY TRIP YOU UP. That one had been so right on it was almost spooky.

She kept scrolling through her horoscopes. Sometimes they seemed to mirror her life exactly. Other times, they were completely off the mark, or she had to twist the meaning to make it make sense. Abby began to wonder, did the horoscopes really match her life? Or had she started making her life match the horoscopes?

Finally, she came to her horoscope from the day before. IF YOU'RE NOT CAREFUL, YOU MAY LOSE SOMETHING IMPORTANT TO YOU.

That was a hard one. *I didn't lose the election,* Abby thought. But she had lost so many other things: Matt, Chelsea, her date to the dance, the respect of some — if not all — of her classmates.

So the horoscope had been wrong. But it had also been right.

Abby put her phone down. She didn't know what to think about horoscopes anymore. She didn't know if they were baloney or true. She didn't know if they were right most of the time, or only some of the time, or only right when you read them the right way.

What she did know now is that she couldn't always depend on it to tell her what to do. She was going to have to start figuring that out for herself.

Abby sighed. It was all such a mess. But the more she thought about it, the more she realized that what bothered her most was Marcus. In his own weird way, he'd been a real friend to her. And she'd let him down.

Suddenly, for the first time in a week, Abby felt like she knew exactly the right thing to do. She had to find a way to make it up to Marcus.

Unfortunately, figuring out what to do turned out to be easier than actually doing it. All that afternoon, Abby tried to catch Marcus in the hallway. But every time he saw her, he scowled and walked in the other direction.

Finally, at the end of the school day, she managed to catch him at his locker. Marcus was busy stuffing schoolbooks into his backpack. He didn't see her until she was right next to him.

"Marcus," Abby said, "listen, I —"

"Save it, Abby," Marcus snapped, cutting her off. "I'm not interested." He snatched up his bag, slammed his locker, and started to walk away.

But in his hurry, he'd forgotten to zip his backpack. As he swung it onto his shoulder, books, pencils, a bruised banana, and other stuff went flying all over the hallway.

Marcus froze, a look of disbelief on his face. For a second, Abby thought he was going to just walk away and leave all his things there. Then with a grunt, he kneeled and started to pick them up.

"Let me help." Abby leaned down next to him and reached for a DVD case that had fallen from his pack.

"Just leave it," Marcus said furiously, brushing her aside. But before he could get to the DVD, another hand reached down and grabbed it.

"This yours, Marcus?" sneered a boy named Chad, waving the case in Marcus's face. Abby's eyes widened when she saw the cover. It was *The Kiss List,* the chick flick she and Marcus had both been discussing in ElectroMania!

"Hey, dudes! Check it out! Marcus likes girl movies!" Chad hollered to a couple of other guys in the hall, waving *The Kiss List* in the air.

Marcus tried to grab the movie out of Chad's hand, but Chad flicked it like a Frisbee to another guy. The guy caught it and waved it tauntingly at Marcus.

"Cut it out," Marcus growled. His face had turned dark red.

The boys continued to toss the movie back and forth over Marcus's head. Other kids in the hall were watching and laughing. Abby couldn't believe this was happening. She'd wanted to make things better with Marcus, and now they were worse!

The next time Chad caught the movie, Abby jumped in front of him. "That's *my* DVD," she snapped. "And if you bust it, you're going to pay for it."

"Oh yeah?" Chad held the movie over Abby's head, just out of her reach. "What's Marcus doing with your movie?"

"I loaned it to his sister," Abby lied. "Marcus was bringing it back to me."

Chad hesitated, with his arm still in the air. He knew he was losing power, but he didn't want to give it up yet. "So how come you know Marcus's sister? Is Marcus your *boyfriend*?" he sneered.

"That's none of your business," Abby snapped. "Give me my movie. My uncle's a cop and if you don't give it back now, I'll have him cite you for stolen property." Another lie! Abby's uncle was an insurance broker. But of course, Chad would never know that.

"Fine. Take your stupid DVD," Chad said, shoving it back at her. "You don't have to freak out about it."

Abby didn't bother to respond. She turned to Marcus and held up the movie. "Thanks for bringing it back."

Marcus stared at her. "Uh, sure," he mumbled.

With a swish of her hair, Abby strode away, still holding the movie. She turned the corner, went out the school doors, and waited.

A few minutes later, Marcus came out of the school wearing his backpack. He stopped when he saw Abby standing there.

"Here," Abby said, holding out the DVD.

Marcus stared at it for a moment. Then he took it from her hand.

"Listen, Marcus," Abby said. "I just wanted to say that I'm sorry. I never meant to hurt your feelings."

Marcus didn't say anything. He took off his backpack, put the DVD case inside, and carefully zipped it up again.

"See you later, Abby," Marcus said. And without another word, he walked away.

⋆ *Chapter Eleven* ⋆

The next day, Chelsea still wasn't talking to Abby. At lunchtime, not knowing who else to sit with, Abby sat down at their usual table. Chelsea made a big point of ignoring her. She spent the whole time talking with Sara and Toshi about the dance.

Abby silently picked at her food. She hadn't felt so left out since she'd come to McKinley. She half wished that she'd gone to the library again, but she couldn't afford to skip lunch that day. The track meet was that afternoon, and Abby knew she didn't stand a chance of making it through her races if she hadn't eaten.

That is, if *I decide to race,* Abby thought. That morning, her horoscope had been particularly discouraging.

LIBRA: SOME DAYS YOU JUST CAN'T WIN. RATHER THAN WEAR YOURSELF DOWN FIGHTING A LOSING BATTLE, CONSIDER SITTING THIS ONE OUT.

A few days before, Abby would have been positive that it meant that she was going to blow the race. She'd have gone straight to Coach Nelson and made up a reason why she had to sit out the track meet.

But now Abby wasn't so sure. The horoscope might be about the race, but maybe it was about something else. Maybe it meant she should have sat at another table for lunch. Or maybe it was telling her to give up on Marcus.

In Ms. Hill's class that morning, Abby had given Marcus an extra-friendly smile. But Marcus had looked away as if he hadn't seen her.

Across the table, Chelsea was going on and on about which color of nail polish she was going to wear that night. Abby sighed. When it came right down to it, she felt like she was in the middle of a lot of losing battles.

But if I sit out the race, Abby thought, going back to the track meet, *I don't stand a chance of winning. And I'd be letting down the rest of the relay team for sure. And if I do race, I still might have a chance,* she reasoned. *Even if it's only a teeny, tiny chance, it's still a chance.*

So what was better, sitting it out or fighting on? In this case, Abby decided, she was going to have to gamble against the stars.

After all, what more did she have to lose?

That afternoon, the sun beat down on the black cinder track behind McKinley. Unlike at the track meet a week before, the day was unseasonably warm — it felt more like August than May. Between events, kids knocked back water and sports drinks, trying to stay cool.

Abby stood at the side of the track, carefully sipping at a bottle of water. She didn't want to drink too fast and risk getting a side cramp. She'd already finished her 100-meter dash, and had come in second in her heat. *Definitely not a win,* Abby thought. *But not a total loss either.*

But the 100-meter dash wasn't her main concern. What she was really worried about was the relay.

Abby set her water bottle down and checked her shoes for what felt like the hundredth time. They were laced up tight and carefully double knotted. She wasn't taking any chances this time.

She was just about to stand, when a familiar pair of running shoes stopped right in front of her feet. Abby looked up. Krista was sneering down at her, her hands planted on her hips.

"Can you tie your shoes wittle Wabbit, or do you need somebody to do it for you?" she asked Abby in a babyish voice.

Abby opened her mouth to reply. Then she shut it.

Sit this one out, said the horoscope in her head.

Abby gave her head a little shake. *Not this time,* she thought.

She stood up, so she was almost nose to nose with Krista. "You know," Abby said as calmly as possible, "if you put half as much energy into running as you do into being nasty to me, your times might actually start to improve."

Krista's nostrils flared. Her jaw worked as she tried to come up with a comeback. Then with a toss of her ponytail, she stormed away.

"Whoa, Abby. Way to give her a taste of her own medicine," said Suz, who'd witnessed the whole scene.

Abby's knees were trembling. She couldn't believe she'd finally stood up to Krista. "Do you think I was too harsh?" she asked.

"She deserved it," said Olu, who'd been standing with Suz. "And anyway, you were right. She needs to start focusing on her own business and leave you out of it."

"I hope it doesn't come back to bite me," Abby said worriedly.

"Hmph." Olu crossed her arms and looked over at Krista, who'd gotten very busy stretching her calves. "If Krista's smart, she'll take it out on the track."

Abby nodded. But Krista wasn't the only thing she was worried about. She felt like she was tempting fate. Would it come back to haunt her in the race?

By the time their event was called, Abby was so nervous she felt queasy. *Some days you just can't win,* the horoscope echoed in her mind.

Don't think about that, Abby told herself as she took her place. *Just keep your eyes on the finish line.*

There was a snap like a firecracker, and the runners were off. Krista instantly shot ahead. But two of the girls from their rival school, Washington, were fast. As they reached the handoff, the three relay teams were tied.

Olu tried to get the lead back, but she was racing two girls who were so tall they looked like they should be in high school. By the time she passed the baton to Suz, their team was falling behind.

"Come on, Suz," Abby whispered, watching her tear down the track, fists pumping. When Suz hit the exchange zone, Abby turned and started to run. Seconds later, she felt the baton land smoothly in her hand.

Abby didn't let herself think. She shifted into gear, like a car changing speeds. The anchor from one of the Washington teams was just ahead of her. Abby put all her power into closing the gap between them.

She was gaining. . . . She had her. . . .

Abby passed her, just as they reached the finish line.

It was so close, Abby wasn't even sure she'd won until she heard the announcer say "McKinley." She turned and saw Coach Nelson screaming, "Yeah, Abby!" The other kids from McKinley were yelling, too. Abby saw Olu and Suz on the side of the track with their fists in the air. Even Krista was smiling.

Abby grinned. She'd done it! *Maybe my luck is finally changing,* she thought.

Or maybe . . .

Maybe it wasn't luck, after all.

As Abby walked off the track, she heard a familiar voice shout, "All right, Abby!" She looked up into the bleachers and saw Marcus with his hands cupped around his mouth.

Marcus was here? Had he come to see her?

Abby waved at him.

Marcus hesitated a moment. Then he gave her a small wave back.

After the track meet was over, Abby caught up with Marcus as he was leaving the bleachers.

"Hey," she said. "That's cool that you made it to the meet."

"Oh." Marcus looked slightly embarrassed. "You know, I have lots of friends on the track team."

"Really?" asked Abby.

"Well, no," Marcus admitted. "Congratulations on your win, by the way."

"Thanks."

The rest of the team was leaving the field. Olu walked past, with her boyfriend, David. He had his arm wrapped around her shoulders. "Hey, good job," he said to Abby as they passed.

"See you at the dance tonight, Rabbit!" Olu called back over her shoulder.

Remembering the dance, Abby's excitement about the race faded. Everyone else would be there celebrating. And she would be home, alone.

"I guess you probably have to go get ready for the dance," Marcus said to her.

Abby shook her head. "I'm not going."

"Really?" Marcus looked surprised. "What about Matt?"

"That was all . . ." Abby paused. How could she explain it? "It was all just a big mix-up. I was doing what I thought I was supposed to do but not what I was *really* supposed to do," she said at last.

"Oh." Marcus nodded as if he understood, though clearly he didn't.

Suddenly, Abby had an idea. "Marcus," she said hesitantly, "would you want to go to the dance together?"

Marcus frowned as if he thought she might be playing a joke on him.

"Just as friends," Abby said quickly. "We could go and hang out."

Marcus squinted at her. "Are you asking me to the dance for real this time?"

Abby smiled. "Yes."

"Okay," Marcus said, nodding. "Then, yes. I'll go to the dance with you."

I can't believe I'm going to the dance with Marcus, Abby thought. *Chelsea is going to freak.* But Abby felt strangely giddy about it. "Cool. I'll pick you up at eight," she told him. "Send me a text with your address. No wait — on second thought, no texts. I'll call you when I get home."

"Deal," said Marcus. "Later, gator."

⋆ Chapter Twelve ⋆

The McKinley cafeteria was as dark as a cave. Colored lights flashed from strobes set up around the room, and music thumped from huge speakers in the corners. The middle of the room was crowded with a mob of dancing kids. When Abby squinted, it almost looked like a nightclub — or what she thought a nightclub might look like, anyway.

"This is a new look for the cafeteria," Abby remarked to Marcus.

"Yeah, imagine if lunch was like this every day," Marcus replied. "It would be awesome."

"Except there aren't any tables," Abby pointed out. "So you'd have to eat and dance at the same time."

"I could handle that," Marcus said.

Abby laughed, remembering his shrimp and gummy bear stunts. "I'll bet you could. But I'm not sure I'd want to watch."

Just inside the door, they spotted Suz and Olu standing with David and Suz's date, a tall curly-haired guy name Rafe. "There's our girl!" Suz shouted, throwing her arms around Abby. "Abby totally rocked at the track meet today," she explained to Rafe. "She took the team home!"

Rafe nodded. "Nice going," he said to Abby.

"Abby, that dress is so cute!" Olu exclaimed. "Where did you get it?"

"Blue Beat," Abby replied with a smile. After the track meet that day, Abby and her mom had done an emergency trip to the mall, and Abby had bought the blue dress she'd found the week before. She'd dressed it up with low heels and a pair of dangly gold earrings she'd borrowed from her mom. Her long hair was loose down her back, and she was wearing just a touch of lip gloss.

She'd been a little worried that it still wouldn't be dressy enough. But now, looking around, Abby saw that kids were dressed in all kinds of things. Some of the girls had on floor-length dresses, others were just wearing skirts and cute tops, and some of the guys had even come in shorts and button-down shirts. It seemed like almost anything was okay. For once, Chelsea had been wrong.

Marcus leaned over to Abby. "I'm just going to say hi to some guys. See you in a minute."

As he headed off to meet his friends, the other two girls looked at Abby in surprise. "Is that your date?" asked Olu. "I thought you were going with Matt Anderson."

"That didn't really work out," Abby told her.

"It's just as well," Olu said. "Matt's nice and all, but he's kind of a knucklehead. Have you ever noticed how he always speaks in one-word sentences?"

Abby laughed. "Yeah. I did."

Suz was still peering over at Marcus. "He's cute," she told Abby.

"Really?" Abby hadn't ever thought of Marcus as *cute*. "We're just friends," she said quickly.

"Rafe and I are just friends, too," Suz told her. "It's nice. Kind of takes the pressure off."

"Yeah." Abby nodded. "I know exactly what you mean."

Just then, a new song came on. "I love this one!" Olu exclaimed, grabbing David's hand and dragging him onto the dance floor. "Catch you later, Rabbit!"

As the girls and their dates left, Abby looked around. She spotted Chelsea standing against the wall with her arms folded. Chelsea was wearing her new green wrap dress, her thick shiny curls cascading over her shoulders. She was staring at the dance floor with a blank expression on her face.

Abby saw Nathan, a few feet away. He was standing around with a bunch of seventh grade guys, pointing out people on the dance floor and laughing.

"Come on, Abby!" Marcus exclaimed, taking her hand. He pulled her into the thick of the moving, bouncing crowd.

Marcus had his own style of dancing, a cross between hip-hop and hoedown, with some air guitar thrown in. Abby swayed a little next to him, trying to keep her moves cool. But Marcus didn't seem to care if his moves were cool. He was clearly having a blast. Finally, Abby threw up her arms, and started doing a goofy dance with him.

"Sweet!" Marcus exclaimed as Abby did a King Tut–style move, bending her arms at right angles and jutting out her neck.

"You're not so bad yourself!" Abby shouted over the music.

Marcus took this as encouragement to get down on the floor and try to do a break-dancing spin on his back. He didn't even make it around once. Abby threw her head back and laughed.

At that moment, she saw Chelsea striding across the cafeteria toward her. And she did not look happy. *Uh-oh,* Abby thought. *She's really going to let me have it now.*

Chelsea grabbed Abby's arm. "Can I please talk to you for a minute?" she hissed into Abby's ear.

Abby nodded reluctantly, and the two girls moved off the dance floor.

As soon as they were out of the crowd, Abby held up a hand. "Look, Chelsea, you don't need to say it," she said. "Yes, I came to the dance with Marcus. So what? I happen to think he's a really nice —"

She broke off. Chelsea's eyes were full of tears.

"What's wrong?" Abby asked.

"Nathan," Chelsea spat, wiping at her eyes. "He's been a jerk all night. He's hardly said a word to me since we got here. All he cares about is hanging out with his friends."

"Oh, Chels." Abby put her arm around her friend's shoulders and gave her a hug. "I'm sorry. I know how excited you were about tonight."

159

Chelsea shook her head, scattering tears across her cheeks. "You were right. I got way too carried away about the whole dance thing. Look," she said bitterly, "I'm still carrying around his stupid boutonniere." She held up a wilted-looking white rose. "He said he wouldn't be caught dead wearing a flower."

Abby took the rose from Chelsea's hand and pulled out the stickpin. Then she tucked the flower behind Chelsea's ear. "There. That looks really nice on you."

Chelsea sniffled and gave a half smile. "I'm sorry I blew up at you," she told Abby.

"I'm sorry, too," Abby said, "About the whole Matt thing, I mean. It's just . . ." She took a deep breath. "I'm not sure I'm ready for dating yet, Chelsea."

"Yeah." Chelsea wiped at her eyes again. "I'm not sure I am either. So . . ." She looked at Abby hesitantly. "Do you think maybe . . . I could dance with you guys? You and Marcus, I mean?"

Abby's eyes widened in surprise. "Of course!" she cried. "Come on!"

Back out on the dance floor, a bunch of kids had formed a circle around Marcus. They were clapping and chanting, "Go, Marcus! Go, Marcus!

Go, Go!" In the center of the crowd, Marcus was dancing like a maniac.

Abby and Chelsea slipped into the circle and started to clap, too. Marcus paused in his crazy moves to give Abby a thumbs-up.

Abby grinned. Then she glanced at Chelsea, who smiled back at her.

"Go, Marcus!" they shouted along with the rest of the crowd. "Go, Marcus! Go! Go! Go! Go!"

check out

ACCIDENTALLY
Fooled

Another

candy apple book . . .

just for you.

"You can see the whole school from up here," I said as I gazed down from the top of the Ferris wheel. A carnival spread out below us, sprawling across the lush green Allington Academy campus. It was completely amazing. Loud music blared from a nearby stage, where bands were scheduled to appear all day. There were tons of fun rides and games, and the school had even set up an enormous half-pipe for skateboarders. "Can you believe how many people showed up? It's so great that the school invites the whole neighborhood to this!"

"Just tell me when we're back on the ground." My good friend Kiwi had her eyes squeezed tight.

"Okay," I said.

"Oh, phew," Kiwi said, opening her eyes. She

let out a shriek when she saw that we were still practically scraping the sky. "That was so mean! I can't believe you did that to me!" She reached for the plastic water pistol on the seat beside her and gave me a playful squirt. "You're pure evil, Amy Flowers!"

I squirted her back. "I *meant*, 'Okay, I'll let you know,' not 'Okay, ride's over.'"

Our car, which was stopped at the top of the wheel, rocked as we moved. Kiwi gave another shriek. "I can't believe you even got me to go on this ride in the first place! You know I'm afraid of heights!"

"What?" I spluttered as a series of short blasts of water hit me in the face. "You're the one who talked *me* into this!" Laughing, I landed a few squirts along her ear and in her long brown hair. We'd won the squirt guns playing a ringtoss game, and I actually didn't mind getting wet. It was March, and already hot in Houston. The water and the air at the top of the Ferris wheel were refreshing.

"You should have known I was talking crazy!" Kiwi insisted. She yelped as the wheel gave a lurch and began to glide toward earth. Kiwi's long tie-dyed sundress fluttered in the breeze as she screamed all the way down.

As we got closer to the waiting line, someone shouted, "That's why you shouldn't let girls go on a Ferris wheel!" Preston Harringford grinned up at me. He was standing beside the metal gate, next in line. "They'll break your eardrums!"

The wheel was still turning. Without thinking, I reached out and squirted him in the face with my water pistol just as our car swooped past him.

The Ferris wheel pulled us up and into the sky, but not before I caught a glimpse of Preston's expression: He was shocked, amused, and — probably for the first time in history — speechless.

In the car beside me, Kiwi's screams had turned to laughter. "Omigosh," she said, giggling. "Did you see his face? That was priceless!" She held up her hand and I gave her a high five.

The Ferris wheel stopped again. This time, we were about halfway down. "This isn't so bad," Kiwi said slowly.

But then the Ferris wheel started up again, and we coasted back toward the ground. "Oh, no!" I exclaimed.

"What?" Kiwi leaned forward so she could see what I was looking at. It was Preston. He was waiting for us in the same spot we'd left him.

And he had a *bucket*.

Kiwi and I shrieked as a tidal wave landed over our heads, completely drenching us.

"Gotcha!" Preston called after us as the wheel turned on and we soared back into the air.

Kiwi was laughing so hard that she could hardly catch her breath.

"I guess I should've thought about the fact that we'd have to go past him again," I admitted as water dripped down my face. But I was giggling, too. Preston had gotten me good that time. Now I'd have to figure out how to get him back!

Read them all!

Accidentally
Fabulous

Accidentally
Famous

Accidentally
Fooled

How to Be a Girly Girl
in Just Ten Days

Miss Popularity

Making Waves

Totally Crushed

Callie for President